SOUL OF EON

EON WARRIORS
BOOK 8

ANNA HACKETT

Soul of Eon

Published by Anna Hackett

Copyright 2020 by Anna Hackett

Cover by Ana Cruz Arts

Edits by Tanya Saari

ISBN (ebook): 978-1-922414-21-2

ISBN (paperback): 978-1-922414-22-9

WHAT READERS ARE SAYING ABOUT ANNA'S ACTION ROMANCE

Heart of Eon - Romantic Book of the Year (Ruby) winner 2020

Cyborg - PRISM Award Winner 2019

Edge of Eon and Mission: Her Protection - Romantic Book of the Year (Ruby) finalists 2019

Unfathomed and Unmapped - Romantic Book of the Year (Ruby) finalists 2018

Unexplored – Romantic Book of the Year (Ruby) Novella Winner 2017

Return to Dark Earth – One of Library Journal's Best E-Original Books for 2015 and two-time SFR Galaxy Awards winner

At Star's End – One of Library Journal's Best E-Original Romances for 2014

The Phoenix Adventures – SFR Galaxy Award Winner for Most Fun New Series and "Why Isn't This a Movie?" Series

Beneath a Trojan Moon – SFR Galaxy Award Winner and RWAus Ella Award Winner

Hell Squad – SFR Galaxy Award for best Post-Apocalypse for Readers who don't like Post-Apocalypse

"Like Indiana Jones meets Star Wars. A treasure hunt with a steamy romance." – SFF Dragon, review of *Among Galactic Ruins*

"Action, danger, aliens, romance – yup, it's another great book from Anna Hackett!" – Book Gannet Reviews, review of *Hell Squad: Marcus*

Sign up for my VIP mailing list and get your *free box set* containing three action-packed romances.

Visit here to get started: www.annahackett.com

CHAPTER ONE

G etting abducted by aliens really sucked.

Commander Kaira Chand strained against her bindings, but the jellylike ooze that kept her wrists and ankles glued to the bench didn't budge.

She flopped back on the hard surface. She *hated* the Kantos.

If one of those bony insectoids came in here, she'd...

Still be stuck. Still be their prisoner.

She turned her head, and her heart knocked in her chest.

She wasn't the Kantos' only prisoner. Medical Commander Thane Kann-Eon was strapped to the bench beside her. Her belly turned over. The Eon warrior was tall and muscular, with dark hair streaked prematurely with gray that only added to his good looks.

His eyes were closed, so she couldn't see his stunning black eyes threaded with strands of green. He'd been unconscious since the Kantos had beaten him during their abduction.

They'd been at the Woomera Range Complex—a weapons testing facility in the Australian desert run by the Australian Air Force. Kaira was the commander in charge of the facility's security. She blew out a breath.

She'd failed. *Big time.*

They'd been at a party to celebrate the success of the StarStorm Project. A Terran scientist, Dr. Finley Delgado, and an Eon warrior, Security Commander Sabin Solann-Ath, had gotten the orbital defense system operational. The array of laser satellites could protect Earth from large-scale Kantos attacks.

While working on the project, Finley and Sabin had fallen in love and mated.

They'd had a lot to celebrate. A party had been thrown at the Complex. One minute Eon warriors and Terrans were mingling, then the next, a small team of Kantos soldiers had attacked.

Kaira prayed everyone was okay. She'd been outside with War Commander Davion Thann-Eon and his pregnant mate Eve, and Thane, when the Kantos soldiers had appeared out of the darkness.

She shoved against her bindings again, drowning in an ugly sense of helplessness. She wasn't going to think about exactly what she and Thane had been doing when the Kantos had attacked them.

She barely knew the warrior, but they'd gone at each other like hormone-riddled teenagers.

That kiss...

She shivered.

Yep, she'd jumped Thane like a...well, definitely not like the sensible, dedicated security commander she usually was. Even with her late husband, she'd never been so out of control. She and Ryan had enjoyed a great sex life, but she'd never been so overcome by desire that she'd jumped him in public.

Kaira sighed. She felt a pang for her husband. He'd been killed two years ago in a training accident. The pain had dulled, but it could still rise up—sharp and gut-wrenching—and surprise her. She'd always miss the sweet, sexy man she'd loved.

"Thane." No response. "*Thane.*"

God, he must be really hurt. The Kantos had put some strange substance on the helian band at his wrist, so he couldn't access his symbiont.

She knew why. The helian that the warriors were bonded with from a young age gave them increased strength, enhanced senses, and amazing abilities.

There was a clank, the door opening, and she turned her head. Their prison was a dank room with faint lighting, and it seemed to be devoid of anything else. She knew they were on a Kantos ship.

Several Kantos soldiers entered.

They kind of reminded her of a humanoid praying mantis. They had four strong, jointed legs, a brown, tough carapace, and armor plates at their shoulders. Four small, yellow eyes dominated their faces.

Another soldier sailed through the door. It was a little taller, skin grayer, and its golden pinprick eyes aimed her way.

Her stomach turned. She'd read files on the Kantos and all the different bugs they had at their disposal. She'd fought alongside Sabin to kill some of them.

She knew this was a Kantos elite.

A buzzing and clicking noise filled the room, and she knew the soldiers were communicating with each other.

The elite moved closer and studied Thane. The alien didn't appear pleased.

This is not War Commander Thann-Eon.

The creepy voice in her head made her grimace. Elites were telepathic.

"No," she said with relish.

Its head swiveled to look at her.

Examine her.

She tensed as two soldiers moved closer. One clawed hand touched her belly. She arched up, fighting against her glue-like bindings.

"Keep your bug hands off me!"

More buzzing filled the room.

You are not with child.

"What? Of course, I'm not." Realization hit. Kaira started laughing and it echoed through the room. The soldiers shifted uneasily.

"You were after Eve and Davion." Kaira laughed harder. "Your bug heads got the wrong couple."

What is your name?

She just grinned at the elite. She was so damn glad that Eve and her baby were safe.

The elite moved fast. It pressed its claws to Kaira's shoulder, digging in.

Tell me your name.

"Fuck you."

The claws sliced into her skin. She hissed. It hurt like hell.

"Tell...them."

She turned her head. Thane's eyes were open. He looked like hell.

He gave her a firm look, and she felt like she could read his mind. If they had any chance of getting out of here, they couldn't do it if they were both injured.

"Commander Kaira Chand," she bit out. "Australian Air Force."

The elite pulled back. *And you, Eon?*

"Medical Commander Thane Kann-Eon."

Of the Rengard. The elite started vibrating, rage pumping off it. There was more intense buzzing, and the soldiers shifted uneasily again.

Suddenly, the elite backhanded one soldier and sent the alien flying. It crashed to the floor.

Kaira felt no sympathy. These alien assholes were targeting Eve and Davion's child—the first Terran-Eon baby.

They could rot in hell.

The elite's eyes glowed. It scanned Kaira, then Thane.

I have no need for the two of you.

It spun on its four legs and strode out.

Oh, God. Her mouth went dry.

The other soldiers filed out, leaving them in silence.

She met Thane's gaze. "So, what happens now?"

The green in his eyes glowed. "Now, I think they'll kill us."

Just great. Her chest locked. Yes, getting abducted by aliens sucked.

THIS WAS A *CREN*-CURSED MESS.

Thane strained against his bindings. The ooze at his wrists and ankles wriggled and flexed, but he couldn't break it. He gritted his teeth. *Cren.*

He needed to get Kaira out of here.

His mate.

Emotion stormed through Thane. He'd never, ever believed he'd mate. Even before mating became rare for the Eon, matings didn't happen in Thane's family. They'd resorted to medical intervention for procreation long before the rest of the Eon had needed it.

People said his family was cursed. There was a terrible story of a long-lost ancestor who'd killed his mate. The most horrible offense for an Eon warrior.

Well, now Thane had a beautiful, impressive Terran mate.

And he wasn't going to let the Kantos kill her.

He strained against his bindings again. He and Kaira barely knew each other. The unheard of had happened—instant mating.

He'd never heard of that happening before. Both of them had been shocked.

Now, he had to get her off this Kantos ship.

Thane kept straining, his veins and muscles popping.

"Thane, you're going to hurt yourself," she whispered furiously.

He kept pushing, keeping Kaira as his motivation.

"Thane!"

With a groan, his wrists moved through the ooze and broke free.

He sat up, shaky, hurting.

He'd watched carefully as the Kantos had used the controls on the bench to lock them in with the bindings. He moved his hands along the bench, found a bump, and pressed the button. The ooze on his ankles melted away.

He wished he could do the same to the black gunk on his helian band. He really needed access to his symbiont. But to release that, he needed to find the antidote.

He swung his legs over the side of the bench and stood. Then he staggered.

"Shit, Thane. Are you okay?"

His vision swam. The pain from his beating made it hard to breathe. Everything hurt. "I'm all right." He crossed the space between the benches. He wanted to touch her, but despite being mated, he knew he hadn't earned that right yet.

He pressed the controls and her bindings melted away. She jerked into a sitting position.

Kaira Chand was tiny compared to him, but had a taut, toned body. Her dark-brown hair was pulled back in a long tail, her skin a smooth brown he wanted to explore, and she had dark, fathomless eyes.

"Thank God." She swung her legs over the side. "Let's blow this joint."

Thane frowned. "What?" The phrase made no sense.

She grinned. "Earth saying. Let's get out of here."

He nodded. That, he could agree with. "First, I need to find the antidote." He lifted his wrist.

She eyed his helian. "Where will we find it?"

"In the ship's labs."

She blew out a breath. "Okay, let's—"

The doors to the room opened. Two soldiers entered, and when they saw Kaira and Thane free, they froze.

"Fuck," Kaira muttered.

A fierce, protective urge rose in Thane.

He kicked at the bench he'd just freed her from. It was made of a hard substance. Not metal, but some sort of resin. He kicked it again and it cracked. On the next kick it broke and he wrenched the leg off and shoved it at Kaira. He broke a second leg off and spun, just as the soldiers rushed at them.

With a cry, Kaira dived into the fight, swinging her bench leg.

So courageous.

Thane swung his weapon. He kicked and hit the Kantos' sharp arm. The alien swung its other arm and Thane dodged.

His hips slammed into a bench and pain rocketed through him.

With a groan, he dodged the Kantos' next strike. He and the soldier traded blows, moving across the room.

He saw Kaira leap onto a bench. She ran along it, the soldier chasing her on the floor below.

She leaped off, and whacked the leg into the soldier's head. The alien rocked back, looking dazed.

Thane's soldier rammed into him. They crashed against another bench.

Thane hammered his fist into the alien's face. It made a frantic buzzing noise.

Suddenly, Kaira leaped onto his Kantos, using her

bench leg to press against the soldier's neck. She jerked it back and the alien kicked.

With all his strength, Thane rammed his bench leg into the soldier's chest. The hard carapace held. He rammed it again. And again.

The soldier's chest cracked. With everything he had, Thane slid his makeshift weapon deep.

The Kantos slumped.

Panting, Thane rose, and Kaira leaped free of the dead Kantos. The other soldier was on the floor, not moving.

"You're a tough fighter, Commander."

She arched a brow. "I was highly motivated."

"Let's get out of here."

"I really like the sound of that."

Thane pried the doors open and glanced out. *Cren.*

He ducked back inside. "The corridor is filled with Kantos."

"Shit," she muttered.

He glanced around. "I think we're close to the Kantos labs." He needed the antidote. Once he had access to his helian, it upped their odds and gave them options. He looked up and his gaze snagged on a grate in the ceiling.

She followed his gaze. "Ventilation ducts." Her nose wrinkled. "How will we get up there?"

The ceiling was high, and Thane considered it carefully.

He grabbed her discarded bench leg from the floor. He hefted it, aimed, and threw it.

It slammed into the grate, knocking it open.

"I'll throw you up." He moved under the grate,

cupped his hands together and gestured with his head. "Run, and put your boot in my palms."

Kaira bit her bottom lip. "How will you get up?"

"I'll jump from the bench."

Her gaze narrowed. "It's too far."

"I have to try. Come on, Kaira. They'll be back soon." He at least wanted her safely out of here.

But she didn't run. She walked to him. "I know you're hurting." She touched his cheek.

That small touch felt so good and he wanted to savor it.

She looked uncertain, like she was fighting herself. Like she didn't want to touch him, but couldn't help herself. She stroked his skin. "Don't you think about not following me into that vent, warrior."

Thane nodded.

She backed up. Then she ran, planted her boot in his palms, and he boosted her high. Such a tough, tiny thing.

She sailed through the air gracefully, caught the lip of the hole in the vent, and pulled herself in.

"Ugh, it reeks in here." Her head popped out. "Your turn, warrior."

He climbed onto the bench. It was a long jump, and his body was already aching.

"Come on, Thane."

He took a deep breath, then ran along the bench and threw himself into the jump.

Cren. He wasn't going to make it.

He extended his arms as far as he could. His fingers brushed metal and he tried to find purchase.

Kaira's hands clamped on his wrists. She grunted,

trying to pull him up. She slid a little, and for a horrible second, Thane was sure they would both come crashing down. Then he gripped the edge of the vent.

Down below, he heard the door opening. *Cren.*

"Come...on." She yanked back.

Ignoring every ache in his battered body, Thane thrust himself upward.

She tugged him into the vent and Thane landed on top of her.

"*Oof.*" The air rushed out of her.

In the gloom, their gazes locked.

Then they heard buzzing below, and they both tensed.

CHAPTER TWO

Kaira heard the Kantos below.

"Quiet." Thane's near-soundless whisper.

She didn't dare move. She prayed the soldiers didn't notice the grate.

Thane's big body pressed into hers. All solid muscle.

Despite the horrible circumstances, it felt damn good to have the man's weight on her.

Shit. She closed her eyes. *How about you focus on surviving the enemy aliens, Chand, and not jumping the hot alien warrior?*

"They're leaving." Thane finally shifted off her. "Now, we search for the labs."

She turned onto her hands and knees to crawl. "Gotcha."

Behind her, she heard him stifle a small groan.

She looked back. "You okay?"

"Fine," he said, in an odd tone.

That's when Kaira realized that her ass was inches from his face.

Jeez. She started crawling, trying to focus on the mission. The ductwork was quite large, so they had room to move. As they crawled along, the smell was *not* pleasant—it stank of bugs and rotting things.

"Stop." He was looking down through a grate, then shook his head.

They kept moving, checking each room that they passed.

"This one," Thane said.

Through the grate, Kaira saw vats of fluid. There were also cocoon-like objects that pulsed gently.

"This is going to be gross, isn't it?" she muttered.

"Highly likely." He carefully opened the grate and peered into the room. "Clear."

He jumped down, landing in a crouch. He rose and held his arms open. "Jump. I'll catch you."

The thought of jumping into Thane's arms made her pulse speed up. She climbed to the edge of the hole, and dropped.

Strong, muscular arms closed around her.

"I've got you." His warm breath puffed against her cheek.

She felt the rumble of his words and licked her lips. "Thanks."

His gaze dropped to her mouth. The green filaments flared brighter.

Then he set her down. "Let's look for the antidote."

They separated. The long benches were covered in... she wasn't sure what. There were small containers bubbling with thick fluids. Everything smelled like month-old garbage mixed with raw sewage. *So disgusting.*

"What the hell are they doing in here?" she mused.

"Concocting new bugs." Thane crouched to look at a white cocoon. As he neared it, it pulsed, something moving inside it.

Kaira grimaced.

"They conduct tests on their enemies," he said. "Find ways to exploit their weaknesses."

"Just when you think they can't get any worse."

Suddenly, Thane froze.

She frowned. "Thane?"

He strode across the lab with barely suppressed fury.

"Thane!" She rushed after him.

Several long, narrow, clear vessels were attached to the wall. Gases swirled around inside, of all different colors.

In the center of each vessel was some sort of crystal.

Most of the crystals were covered in what looked like mold spots and furry growth. The crystals were twisted and black.

"Hey." She grabbed his arm. "Talk to me."

"They're helians." He looked away, muscle ticking in his jaw. "Helians may not have bodies like ours, but they're sentient. They live. They want to use their abilities. That's why they bond with the Eon. The Kantos are experimenting on them. Killing them."

God. She looked at the vessels. "Can you tell what they're doing to them?"

"No. I need my helian."

"Let's find the antidote." Determination filling her, she strode through the lab.

They checked boxes, looked on every surface.

Dammit. Where the hell would the bugs keep this?

Then she spotted a small container with a heavy lock. "Thane?" She lifted the box.

He hurried over and smashed the lock. He flipped open the lid. Relief crossed his hard features. "This is it."

He pulled out a small vial and tipped the fluid onto his helian band. It ate away at the black ooze.

He dragged in a breath and she saw the way he straightened.

"Okay?" she asked.

He nodded. His black-scale armor formed. It flowed up his arm and across his broad chest. *Amazing.*

"Kaira, you should form armor, too. It'll offer you protection." His face was unreadable. "I'm able to share my armor with my mate."

She stiffened. "I'm not interested in mating."

He stayed silent.

"My husband—"

Thane sucked in a breath. "You're married?"

"Widowed. My husband died two years ago."

"I'm sorry."

She heard the sincerity in his voice. She looked at her boots, fighting the emotions churning around in her gut. "It nearly broke me. Losing the man I loved." She met Thane's gaze. "I will *never* love again. I'm fine, just as I am."

Thane inclined his head. "We can discuss this after we escape."

Right. Escape had to come first. She nodded.

"But it makes sense to take the protection of my armor."

Damn. He was right. She gave him another nod.

A second later, black scales flowed off his armor and over her body. The armor covered her, snug and tight. She stroked it, feeling how flexible and strong it was.

Thane was already back at the helian testing tanks. He pressed his palm to the first container and sucked in a breath.

"How bad is it?" she asked.

He shook his head and moved to the next one. Inside, the crystal was withered and an ugly brown color.

"These helians are dying." Anger and sorrow mixed in his voice.

He was a doctor. It must cut him deep to see this. To see a living life form, like the one he was bonded with, suffer.

"It looks like the Kantos are developing some sort of pathogen that targets helians," he said. "That's what is in the gas."

Kaira gasped, and eyed his helian band.

His jaw worked. "The Kantos came after Airen, the second commander of the *Rengard.* They believed that something about her female physiology would make it easier to disrupt the bond between warrior and helian." He glared at the testing tanks. "It looks like they are closer than ever to succeeding. We need to get off the ship."

"How do we do that?"

"We steal a swarm ship. We need to get to the main hangar."

"Oh, okay, let's get—"

The doors to the lab opened.

They both dropped down behind a bench.

A bug entered. It was large and took up the entire doorway.

The alien was bright green, with spikes covering its legs. Two large, purple eyes topped its head.

The creature lifted its head, sniffed, then screeched.

The sound was loud, battering Kaira's eardrums. She winced and saw Thane grimace.

Then the bug charged into the lab.

THE BUG CRASHED through the room, knocking benches over.

Cren. Thane's fingers curled into his palm. They needed to get out.

Objects tumbled to the floor, and a nostril-searing smell filled the room. Beside him, Kaira gagged. He grabbed her arm and tugged her along the bench.

The bug lifted its front legs and screeched again. Thane morphed his sword, relishing the renewed connection to his helian.

"Stay down." Then he leaped over the bench and landed in front of the bug.

It skittered forward and Thane slashed. The creature screeched. He dropped down, slid under the body of the bug, and ran the sword into the creature's soft underbelly.

The alien went wild, its thorn-covered legs slamming down.

Thane rolled, and a leg caught him, winding him. The spikes tore against his armor.

"Hey!"

Kaira. He looked up.

She'd managed to morph a sword as well. "Come on!"

Cren. He'd told her to stay down.

The bug charged. She grabbed a small, empty vat off a bench and threw it at the alien. It smashed into its head.

The creature skidded, shaking its head wildly. Without pause, Kaira rushed at it, and stabbed it with her sword.

The alien made a deafening noise and slashed out with its front legs. One of its legs hit Kaira, sending her flying

No. Thane leaped up.

He jumped onto the back of the bug. It tried to buck him off, but he held on, and raised his sword high, then he rammed it down.

It connected with a crack, and he worked it through the hard, green shell. Darker green blood dripped down the bug's side.

Grunting, he kept pushing. He had to keep Kaira safe. Finally, his sword hit something vital.

With another wild noise, the bug collapsed beneath him and he leaped off. "Kaira!"

She leaned against a bench, holding her side. "I'm okay."

"Let me see." He strode toward her.

"I told you—"

He touched her side. "I'm the doctor." He probed. She hissed.

"You might have some broken ribs."

"Just bruised. I've broken ribs before, and it felt worse than this. Thane, we can't stop now."

Cren, she was right. He nodded. By the warriors, the urge to see her safe was overwhelming.

A buzzing noise filled the corridor.

They both stiffened.

"Kantos soldiers are coming," she said.

"We need to barricade the door."

"The bench," she suggested.

They both pressed their hands to one of the long workbenches, and together they pushed.

Thane gritted his teeth. "Harder."

The bench screeched as it moved across the floor, sliding and ramming against the door.

He spun. "We need a way out."

"Back into the ducts?"

He scanned the lab. "Agreed."

They pushed another bench right beneath the open grate. Kaira climbed up and was about to jump, then she stilled.

"Kaira?"

"Wait. I hear something."

Thane heard it, too. A skittering sound in the vent.

He circled Kaira's waist and yanked her off the bench.

Tiny bugs poured out of the vent opening, like a dark waterfall.

"Fuck," she breathed.

"Back up."

They retreated, and watched as insects flowed into

the room. They landed on one of the experiments, and instantly devoured it.

"Double fuck," she breathed.

Thane gritted his teeth. He formed a flamethrower and waved flames across the sea of bugs. They shriveled and died, but more continued to pour out of the vent.

"Thane, the door?"

There was a heavy pounding on the doors. They vibrated under the force. The Kantos would break through soon.

Cren.

"We need another way out," he said.

"I'm looking."

There was no fear in her voice. No hysteria. Just quiet competence.

"Here! There's a grate in the wall." She crouched.

Thane kept pouring flames onto the bugs.

Kaira kicked the vent. "Come on." She kicked again. Then she dropped down, and kicked the grate with both feet.

Some bugs flew onto Thane. They were tiny, but they nipped at his arm, hair, and skin with sharp teeth. It felt like knives. He batted them off.

"Got it!" Kaira yelled.

Thane sprayed fire again.

He glanced back and saw the grate bent inward.

With a giant crash, Kantos soldiers smashed through the door.

"Go!" Thane yelled.

Kaira leaped in, feetfirst.

Thane did one more spray of fire, then dived after her.

The vent was near vertical. He slid fast.

Cren. Was Kaira okay?

He picked up speed. He hoped to the warriors that the bugs were not pouring in after them.

Suddenly, he shot out of the vent.

He sailed through the air, then landed with a splash. Sitting up, he saw he was in a square room with smooth, metallic walls. Faint light filtered down from some lights above.

"Thane." Kaira sloshed over to him.

The space was filled with trash and knee-deep liquid. The rancid, rotting smell was near overpowering.

"Are you all right?" he asked.

She nodded, then gagged. "The smell—" She turned and retched.

The trash had a lot of organics in it. "This looks like waste, along with refuse from the lab experiments."

She gagged again.

Thane commanded his helian to form helmets for both of them.

Once they'd formed, he watched Kaira breathe deeply. "Thank God."

He took a deep breath of clean air and grabbed her arms. "Better?"

She smiled at him. "Much. Thanks."

He stroked his hands up her arms. She sucked in a breath, then she was in his arms. Her helmet pressed against his chest.

He wrapped his arms around her. "You're all right now."

She gave a hiccupping laugh and held onto him. "How is standing knee-deep in God knows what okay?"

"Well, the bugs didn't follow us."

She lifted her head. Her beautiful dark eyes gleamed through the helmet. "That just worries me more."

Hmm, it worried him, too. He pulled her close again. But right there, in that second, they were both alive, and that was what he wanted to celebrate.

His mate—even if she didn't want to be his mate—was in his arms.

CHAPTER THREE

This place was gross.

Kaira eyed the debris floating in the brown water and grimaced. At least the smell had reduced now, thanks to the helmet. She pressed harder to Thane's strong body.

Just a few seconds longer. He made her feel less alone.

Finally, she made herself pull back and straighten.

He shot her a warm look, and it made her insides tingle. It also set off alarm bells. She liked it. Too much.

She wasn't getting in deep with a man again. Especially a gorgeous alien warrior.

"So," she said, "what now?"

Thane eyed the vent they'd dropped out of. "I'm not sure."

Kaira sloshed across the space. The stench still burned in the back of her nostrils. "There are other vents. Maybe we can climb up a different one?" She turned and eyed the water again. "Let's just hope there isn't some creature living in here, and that the walls don't start contracting."

Thane's brows rose.

She smiled. "Old, classic, sci-fi movie on Earth. Intrepid heroes and heroines caught in a ship's trash compactor."

He moved to the wall, running a gloved hand over it. "I don't think this is a compactor."

"So how do the Kantos get rid of all this?"

"I believe they dump it into space."

Great. She had to ask. Kaira checked the walls as well. All the vents were too high for them to reach.

She saw something move in the water and she stiffened. "*Thane*, there's something down here."

"I'm detecting a few life signs."

Her stomach clenched. *Just wonderful.*

"They aren't large," he added.

She saw the back of a creature slide through the water, then disappear in the murk. It reminded her of a small crocodile.

She sloshed over to Thane. A sense of hopelessness washed over her.

She didn't want to die.

Especially not in this horrible place.

"Kaira?"

She blinked. "Sorry, just having a moment."

He gripped her arm and squeezed. "That's perfectly normal."

She gave a laugh that wasn't filled with any humor. "You know, when my husband died, a part of me wanted to die, too."

"Kaira." Thane's voice was laced with sympathy.

"All our dreams, everything we'd planned, our life together was just...gone." She closed her eyes. "I figured my life should be over, too."

He pulled her against his chest and she grabbed onto him.

"But right now, I don't want to die, Thane. I want to live."

She didn't die with Ryan. She'd thrown herself into her work the last year to the exclusion of everything else. It was an uncomfortable realization that she'd stopped living and had just barely been getting by.

"You aren't going to die." Thane's voice was fierce. "I won't let that happen."

"I'm glad you're with me," she murmured.

He touched her helmet. The man had beautiful hands—strong, with long fingers.

"Now, let's get out of here," he said.

She gave a firm nod.

Something splashed in the water. They both swiveled and formed swords.

Well, she was never going to get used to this helian thing, but it was starting to get easier.

The scaled creature rose again, then launched through the water, lightning-fast.

Thane cursed and Kaira lifted her sword.

All she could see was an open mouth, full of needle-sharp teeth. She slashed.

The creature screeched and thrashed. Thane's long sword speared down through the creature.

It went still, floating in the dirty water.

"Back up," Thane warned, pulling his sword free.

They backed up.

Suddenly, the water started to churn. Drawn by blood, other things attacked the dead creature.

"Oh, God." Kaira grimaced as the feeding frenzy began.

Thane pulled her back farther. She really, really wanted off this ship.

"I'll see if I can scale the wall up to one of the vents." He pointed to the closest one. "We need to get to the hangar. Stealing a swarm ship is still our best bet." He gave her a faint smile that lit up his handsome face. "Or we can try the escape pods, like Sabin and Finley did."

Kaira made a sound. "Float around space in the equivalent of a coffin? No, thanks."

"Like I said, a swarm ship would be better."

"The Kantos will come after us."

"Yes, but if we're in a swarm ship, it's equipped with weapons. We'll have a better chance."

She nodded. "Let's—"

An earsplitting screech of alarms started blaring.

"What the hell?" she yelled over the cacophony.

Thane's jaw was a hard line as he looked around.

That's when Kaira realized something.

The feeding frenzy had stopped. The half-eaten carcass was floating, green blood spreading around it.

"Where did they go?" she asked.

Thane's arms clamped around her and she looked up at him.

"Thane?"

"Hold on," he growled.

There was a giant *whoosh* of sound.

A scream lodged in Kaira's throat as they were sucked out into space.

No. Fuck.

She clung to Thane as they tumbled, end-over-end, and debris whooshed past them. She got a view of the Kantos ship, then nothing but the blackness of space.

DEBRIS STREAMED PAST THEM.

Thane pulled Kaira close. He generated a pulse of propulsion from his helian to slow their spin.

Thank the warriors they were in armor, and his helian was providing air for them.

"God." Her fingers flexed on his arms.

They finally stopped and he steadied her. They both looked up, watching the Kantos ship slowly moving away from them.

Leaving them hanging in space with no planets nearby.

"Jesus, what do we do now?" she said.

Thane's mouth firmed. "We need to find a way to contact the *Rengard*, or another Eon ship."

"Thane, how?" She turned her head. "There's *nothing* out here."

"I'm not sure yet." He had no emergency beacon. They were only supplied to warriors on missions. He'd been on Earth for a celebration. He hadn't expected to be abducted by the Kantos.

"Right now, let's put some distance between us and

the Kantos." He generated more propulsion from his helian. The blast helped them fly away from the battle-cruiser.

"Okay."

"Keep your arms by your side," he said.

She adjusted her stance to be more aerodynamic. "Sorry. I've only been in space a couple of times. During my space modules at the Air Force Training Academy. And once I visited my dad on his ship."

"Your father is Space Corps?"

A pause. "Was. His ship was destroyed by the Kantos."

There was a tremble in her voice.

"I'm sorry. You lost your husband and your father."

"Yes. Thanks." Her voice was husky.

Thane looked ahead. All he could see was the dense black of space. No stars or planets in view. Frustration rose. He kept his arm tight around Kaira. He had no way to protect her.

They were stuck. Helpless.

"Thane... Hey." She tapped the side of his helmet.

He looked at her.

"We're in this together," she said. "Whatever happens."

He nodded. "I know our mating was a shock, and not what you wanted, but I'm thankful."

Her lips parted. "You don't even know me."

"Sabin spoke highly of you. And he rarely speaks highly of anyone. I don't need to spend weeks with you to know you're honorable, kind, and good at your job."

Even through the helmet, he saw the light flush in her cheeks.

"The kind of mate any man would be honored to have." He dragged in a breath. "I am sorry this mating was thrust on you."

"You can't have wanted this instant mating either," she said.

"Mating has become rare for the Eon, so it's revered."

"Oh. Why has it become rare?"

"We aren't sure. Lots of Eon doctors and scientists have studied the problem. Mating is required for us to be fertile, so conception rates decreased rapidly. We switched to focus on medical ways to allow couples to conceive." He paused. "Now, with so many Eon-Terran matings, our scientists are trying to work out why. Perhaps because of an influx of new genetic material."

"And instant matings? Like what happened to us?"

"I've never heard of it happening before."

"Wow." She looked away, then back. "How did it happen for your parents?"

Thane cleared his throat. "My parents aren't mated. They are in a committed relationship, akin to your marriages on Earth."

"I see."

"In fact, there haven't been any matings in my family for generations."

"Why?"

His jaw worked. "No one knows. Some say my family is cursed."

"That doesn't sound like a very Eon-like thing to believe."

He tightened his hold on her. "I never, ever expected to find my mate."

Her eyes widened. "But you wanted it."

More than anything. "Every warrior does." He didn't say anymore. He would never force Kaira into something she didn't want. "We need to focus on finding a way to contact my warship."

"I'm sorry, Thane. I have no idea how the hell we can do that." She worried her bottom lip. "Can your helian generate a signal?"

"Not very far."

"Damn." She looked over his shoulder and tensed.

He swiveled.

The Kantos ship was turning back.

Cren. "They realized what happened to us."

"Shit."

He pushed for more speed from his helian, but he knew it was futile. They couldn't outrun a ship and they had nowhere to go.

Kaira looked back. "The Kantos are gaining."

Thane saw a shuttle slide out the side of the ship. It had a bug-like design, with a bulbous, brown hull.

"Incoming." *By Ston's sword*, there was *nothing* he could do to stop them being recaptured. He stopped the propulsion. They stopped and turned to face the incoming shuttle.

"Hey." Her hand tightened on his. "It's okay."

"I want to keep you safe."

"I'm good at looking after myself."

He felt his lips curve. He had no doubt about that.

"We're in this together." Her fingers squeezed his.

"Together," he repeated.

The shuttle drew closer. Several Kantos soldiers flew out of the side, their legs tucked behind them.

"We don't have to go easily, do we?" she asked silkily.

He grinned. "No."

Her smile was sharp. "Good."

They both formed swords.

The Kantos flew closer and Thane attacked.

He'd trained in space fighting. He saw Kaira found it difficult, but she attacked with gusto, swinging her sword wildly.

Thane hacked up one soldier. He saw more fly out of the Kantos shuttle.

Cren. Soon, they'd be overrun.

One Kantos hit Kaira and she flew backward. Thane caught her.

Suddenly, they were surrounded by soldiers, their sharp arms pointed at them.

Cren. He ground his teeth together.

He retracted his sword.

Kaira sighed and did the same.

A soldier moved in and hit Thane in the back of the neck, the blow hard.

Darkness descended. The last thing he heard was Kaira shouting his name.

CHAPTER FOUR

They sat in a tiny cell aboard the Kantos shuttle. Kaira shifted on the hard cold floor, Thane's head resting in her lap.

Their helmets were retracted now, and she stroked his hair. The Kantos had covered his helian in goop again. Their armor was gone and she could hardly believe she was still wearing the wide-legged pants and fitted white shirt she'd worn to the party. It felt like a lifetime ago.

Thane still hadn't regained consciousness after the vicious blow to his head.

"Come on, Thane." She swallowed the lump in her throat.

They'd been traveling for a while. She'd expected to dock with the battlecruiser, but they hadn't. She stroked his cheekbone. She had no idea what the Kantos had in store for them.

Right now, she felt horribly alone. She tried again to rouse her warrior. "Wake up, Thane."

He stirred.

"Thane?"

Thane's extraordinary eyes opened. He blinked, then reached up and cupped her cheek. "Kaira."

"We're fine. On the Kantos shuttle."

She helped him sit up. He frowned, gingerly probing the back of his neck with his fingertips. "We haven't docked with the battlecruiser yet?"

She shook her head. "You've been out for about one Earth hour. Thane, I don't think we're docking."

Worry crossed his face.

Where the hell were the Kantos taking them?

"Is your head okay?" she asked.

"Fine. Just some minor swelling. Your ribs?"

"They're throbbing, but nothing's broken."

"Once I can free my helian, I can share some healing ability with you."

Nice. The whole mating thing might freak her out, but she wasn't going to complain about the benefits in this situation. "So, what do we do now?"

He took her hand and twined their fingers. "There's not much we can do but wait, and be ready."

Kaira blew out a breath, ruffling her hair. "I hate waiting."

He smiled. It looked damn good on him. "I'm pretty good at waiting. As a doctor, patience is a valuable skill."

She wasn't sure why she did it. She just felt warmth in her belly, and the need to be connected to him. She cupped his face, leaned forward, and pressed her mouth to his.

He made a deep, raw sound, his arm snaking around her.

Her lips parted, and his tongue slid against hers.

Oh, boy. She kissed him deeper and moaned into his mouth.

He dragged her into his lap and she straddled him. He tasted like heaven.

She slid her hands into his thick, gray-streaked hair. It felt like silk. *More.* In Thane's arms, she was just a woman who needed a man.

He cupped the back of her neck and kissed her deeply. A hot, possessive caress.

Then suddenly, he lifted his head and broke the kiss.

Kaira sucked in air, fighting to get her brain firing.

"We're descending," he said.

Oh, shit. She'd been so lost in him that she hadn't even noticed.

Where the hell were they?

"Be ready for anything," he said.

She nodded. *Time to get her unruly hormones under control.*

The shuttle landed, and Thane pulled her up to stand.

It wasn't long before the door to their cell opened. Two soldiers stood in the doorway.

One prodded her and Thane out the door.

With one Kantos in front of them, and one behind, they were shuffled through a short corridor and toward the back of the shuttle. A large door was open.

They were shoved outside.

Kaira blinked at the bright light. Two huge suns—one yellow and one red—dominated the sky.

Thane stayed close to her.

Ahead of them lay a deep valley. The ground was rocky—a dark, black rock with a silver shine to it. In the distance, dramatic, spiky slabs of rock cut into the sky.

They stood on a flat area where the Kantos shuttle had landed. There was no vegetation, but in the distance, she saw pockets of thick, jungle-like greenery.

What was this planet?

An elite stood with a group of other soldiers, and turned to face them.

Welcome to Crolla.

The name didn't mean anything to her. Thane's face didn't change, so it seemed he didn't know of it either.

This is a Kantos proving planet. You're deep in Kantos space.

Her belly tightened.

The elite's eyes glowed. *This is where we train our young soldiers.*

Okay, that didn't sound great.

If our juveniles survive Crolla, they are assigned to battlecruisers.

Survive. Kaira glanced at the terrain. What horrors were hiding out there?

It was decided that instead of executing you, we would give our juveniles a chance to hone their skills hunting an Eon warrior and a Terran.

Kaira pressed her lips together. *Great.* They got to be prey for baby Kantos.

I do not believe you will survive, Terran and Eon. If the juveniles don't kill you, the wildlife will. I will grant you a few small things. The elite nodded.

A solider shoved a small water bottle at Kaira.

It will only prolong your suffering.

Then several soldiers surrounded them, eyes glowing. One moved forward and quickly slapped the antidote on Thane's helian band.

I wouldn't want to make your death too quick.

With that, the elite flowed back toward the shuttle.

Asshole. Kaira glared.

A soldier prodded them. She jerked, ready to attack, but Thane grabbed her arm and pulled her away.

Somewhere in the distance, a creature roared.

She tensed.

"Let's go," Thane said.

She followed him and they broke into a run.

Now it was a race for survival.

"SO, this is just one big planet filled with things that want to kill you," Kaira said.

Thane turned his head. "I'm guessing that's an accurate summary."

They were jogging down a rocky slope. He'd shortened his stride a little, but despite her small size, Kaira was easily keeping pace with him.

"It reminds me of our Hunter planets," he said.

"I've read about those. Synthetic planets where you Eon warriors go to kill a bunch of genetically engineered creatures."

"Where we go to test our skills."

She snorted. "Sure. Doesn't matter what planet males are from, the desire to fight lives on."

His lips twitched. "Hunter planets also change biomes. The landscape changes every few hours."

Kaira groaned. "I hope to hell this planet doesn't do the same."

"As far as I know, the Kantos don't have that technology."

They both scanned the inhospitable terrain.

"No, but they can breed nasty things," Kaira said.

He could see more pockets of vegetation dotted across the rocky landscape. Each pocket looked different—some with more jungle trees and tangled vines. Others thickets of blackened trees with bare limbs.

"We need a plan," she said.

He admired Kaira's straightforward approach and intelligence. He scanned the ground again.

"See that larger, rocky outcrop in the distance?" He pointed to a tall, tower-like, rock structure. The horizon was hazy in the distance, but he could just make out mountains beyond the outcrop.

She shook her head. "My eyesight isn't as good as yours."

"If we can make it there, we'll have a better view, and we'll be able to see more from that outcrop."

Her mouth firmed. "Let's do it."

They kept jogging.

The distant howl of a predator filled the air.

"I'd kill for a hot shower and a bowl of my grand-mother's beef vindaloo. And her garlic naan."

"These are types of food?"

"Yes. From the country where she was born. India.

Vindaloo is a spicy curry." A faint smile crossed Kaira's lips. "Might be too much for your Eon palate."

"My helian means I can ingest a larger range of food than you."

Her grin widened. "I don't know, warrior. My grand-mother's vindaloo is eye-watering."

"You're close to your family?"

She nodded. "I see my mom regularly. She lives in Adelaide in Australia. Not too far from Woomera. I see her often, especially since my father died." There was grief in her voice.

"Siblings?"

"I have a younger sister. She's a sound engineer. You?"

"An only child. I'm close to both my parents."

"We are going to get off this rock and see our families again, Thane."

He nodded. He'd do everything he could to keep her safe and get her home.

"I'm really glad you're with me." She grabbed his hand.

"Me too," he murmured.

They got closer to a patch of dense, jungle-like vege-tation. They paused and she pulled out their meager supply of water. He took it and sniffed to check it was drinkable, then handed it to her.

"It's safe."

She took a small sip from the bottle. "Until we find another water source, we can't waste it." She studied the wall of green. Tangled vines in green, black, and yellow dangled everywhere. The dense trees made it hard to see very far.

"Do we go through or around?" she asked.

The rock tower they were aiming for was on the other side.

"Through is faster." Thane frowned. "But we have no idea what's inside."

Suddenly, a flock of bird-like creatures took flight from the trees, squawking loudly.

In the center of the jungle, trees started shaking violently. A loud growl echoed.

"Around," Thane said.

Kaira nodded. "Definitely around."

They skirted the vegetation, falling into a jog again.

They hadn't gone far when his helian pulsed. He scanned behind them.

"What is it?" she asked.

"I'm not sure yet—"

"Thane. It's better if I know. You don't need to protect me."

No, she was strong and well able to protect herself. He felt a sense of pride. She was an incredible mate. Whatever happened, he was proud that she was his. If only for a short time.

"We're being hunted," he told her.

"What?" She looked back. "I don't see anything."

"I don't either, but my helian senses it."

She swallowed.

"Let's keep moving. We don't want to alert whatever it is that we know it's there."

They kept going. Then Thane sensed vibrations under his feet and spun.

Out of the hazy fog, a pack of large shapes thundered toward them.

Thane formed his sword.

"What the hell?" Kaira muttered, forming her own sword.

The predators got closer, and Thane tensed.

"Fuck," Kaira said. "They look like black polar bears crossed with wolves."

The large bodies ran quickly on all four legs. Instead of fur, they were covered in black, leathery skin. Two wicked fangs, as long as his forearm, flanked their jaws.

"With a dash of sabretooth tiger." Kaira lifted her sword.

"Run for the outcrop. I'll distract them to give you a head start."

Her dark eyes narrowed. "Nice try, warrior. I'm *not* running, and I'm not leaving you."

Cren.

The creatures thundered closer.

One reared, showing the sharp claws on its paws.

Thane ran forward, and leaped into the air, lifting his sword.

Protect Kaira. That was his only priority.

CHAPTER FIVE

K aira watched Thane's powerful body fly through the air, sunlight reflecting off his sword. He hit the lead beast, sending it skidding across the ground with a growl.

A huge bear-wolf landed in front of her and snarled.

"Come on, then." She ignored the wicked fangs and braced herself.

It charged.

Kaira dodged and swung her sword. The tip of her blade raked the creature's side, leaving a jagged, red line.

Enraged, it spun. Several others were close by, pacing, watching the fight for their turn.

Maybe the alpha pair got first dibs. *Sorry, vicious alien creature, no snacks for you today.*

The creature came at her again and she slashed with her sword.

Thane leaped in from the side. Together, they forced the bear-wolf back.

"Will the rest of the pack attack?" she asked.

"Eventually."

The creatures were pacing, looking restless and hungry.

"We need to keep moving," she said. "We need to get to that outcrop."

Another creature slunk closer and snarled.

Thane charged it.

He was fearless. She sucked in a breath. God, he was something. She could watch him fight all day.

He slashed at the creature, leaping high and attacking again.

There was a growl behind her and she spun.

A smaller, leaner bear-wolf was stalking her. It snarled. She guessed it was a juvenile.

She spun her sword in her hand, getting a better grip. The beast charged, its mouth open, showing its huge teeth.

Hell. Kaira dodged, almost tripping on some loose rocks.

The creature spun and lunged at her.

She dropped low and it sailed over her head. Its skin was black like ink. Jumping up, she sprinted away. She needed room to maneuver.

She heard it coming after her. She dived to the side and rolled.

Ignoring the hard impact with the ground, the rocks biting into her, she leaped back to her feet.

The bear-wolf bore down on her.

She rocked on the balls of her feet. *Come on, then.*

"Kaira!"

Thane, sword dripping with blood, sprinted toward her.

She blocked him out and focused on the alien creature.

It raced closer and roared.

Kaira ran...straight at it.

She jumped and grabbed a handful of loose skin on its neck. She leaped onto the creature's back, giving a thousand mental thank yous for her horseback riding lessons as a kid.

She clenched her legs onto the animal, holding tight. It bucked and spun, then dashed away.

Toward the outcrop.

It required all her strength to hold on. Her bones rattled, and the bear-wolf leaped into the air. She leaned forward.

It skidded to a stop and she almost flew off.

It turned in an agitated circle.

The rocks loomed above them. When she glanced back, she saw Thane sprinting toward her, the rest of the pack chasing him.

The bear-wolf she was riding reared, bucking her off.

Shit. Kaira landed hard, the wind knocked out of her. She rolled onto her hands and knees.

And saw the bear-wolf running at her.

Oh, fuck. She rolled.

It almost trampled her. It reared up, and slammed its paws down, missing her by inches.

Her heart was pounding like an out-of-control jackhammer, the beast's low growl was loud in her ears. It slashed out and caught her shoulder. It burned.

The bear-wolf reared again and she rolled the other way. Paws slammed into the rock right beside her head.

"Hey!"

Thane's shout made the creature lift its head. Thane attacked it.

"*Go*, Kaira," he yelled.

She rolled away.

"Climb the outcrop. I'll be right behind you."

She saw the rest of the pack running at them. Fast.

Shit.

She ran to the rock wall, gripped a crack, and started climbing.

High. She needed to go high. She was pretty sure the bear-wolves could jump a reasonable distance.

She wedged her foot into another crack, gripped the small ledge, and hauled herself upward. Then she slipped. *Crap.* She caught herself, gritted her teeth, and kept going.

Finally, she pulled herself onto a flat rock outcrop. Panting, she looked over the edge.

"Thane!"

Her throat closed. The wounded creature was still attacking him. The others were getting closer.

What if he got hurt? Killed? "Thane, now!"

He stabbed the alien beast, and its back legs collapsed. Then he sprinted toward the outcrop.

The other creatures were gaining.

"Come on, warrior," she whispered, her heart in her throat.

He leaped, and hit the rock face. Then he climbed.

The closest creature was readying to leap. Kaira grabbed a loose rock, lifted it, and heaved it.

It flew past Thane and hit the bear-wolf's head. It dropped to the ground with a yelp.

Thane reached her, and she grabbed his arm and helped him over the edge.

Thank God.

The creatures milled down below. Contemplating them.

Thane stood, breathing heavily. Then, the first bear-wolf leaped, trying to climb up the wall.

"Oh, shit," Kaira said. "You've got to be kidding me."

Thane lifted his arm. His sword was gone and a large blaster formed.

Wow. She needed to work out how to do that.

He aimed. A ball of green energy hit the climbing beast.

It fell backward and crashed to the ground.

Thane fired again and again. The creatures scattered, bounding away.

"Thank God." Kaira pressed against Thane and he wrapped an arm around her.

THANE'S BLOOD still pumped wildly through his veins. He sat on the rocky outcrop, holding Kaira close to his side.

They were safe. *For now.*

"Jesus." Kaira scraped a hand over her face. "That was intense."

"Are you all right?" he asked.

"Yeah."

He suspected that was just a small taste of what this planet would offer them. He spotted a scratch on her armor. Through the tear, he glimpsed the skin on her shoulder and blood.

"Your shoulder." He leaned over and touched it.

She winced. "I don't think it's too bad. Will the armor repair?"

He nodded. From what he could see, the scratch was thankfully shallow. His helian would help her body heal it.

She sucked in a breath.

"It hurts?" he asked.

"No." Her voice lowered.

He slid his hand to her neck and felt the fast tick of her pulse. Then he looked into her eyes and felt a stir of heat in his gut.

Desire burned there, hard and hot. His own need flared to life. He was so glad she wasn't hurt and alive.

"Thane." Her gaze ran over his face.

Then she closed the gap between them.

As soon as her lips touched his, Thane wrapped his arms around her. She felt so good.

She cupped his head, hummed, and deepened the kiss.

He felt a deeper heat. *Cren*, was this the mating fever stirring?

Her tongue stroked his and he gripped her hips. "You're so beautiful, Kaira," he murmured against her lips.

Beautiful. Brave. Tough. His mate was magnificent.

She made a needy sound, then she stiffened and wrenched away.

Hurriedly, she scrambled to her feet. "I'm sorry. I can't do this."

Thane's hands curled into fists. He fought for control. "I'll never hurt you, Kaira. Never force you."

"I know. I want you." She blew out a breath. "But...I can't get involved. I *can't*."

He rose, emotions tearing at him. She'd made it clear that she didn't want him or their mating. It felt like claws tearing at his gut, worse than anything this planet's creatures could do to him.

He looked at the ground. "I understand." Then he met her gaze.

She took a step toward him, then stopped herself. "It isn't personal, Thane. I just can't..." She swallowed. "We need to focus on getting off the planet."

He pulled in a deep breath. She was right. Survival had to be their main focus.

"What now?" she asked, trying to sound businesslike.

Trying to shift his mind off his desire for her, he scanned the landscape. There were no signs of the predators that had attacked them, but there were some large ominous-looking shadows in the distance.

There was also the mountain range, just jagged shadows, and more slab-like rocks spearing into the air.

Then he noticed something.

"See that?" he pointed.

Kaira squinted and shook her head. "I can only make out vague shadows."

"On the nearest mountain. There's a cocoon-like structure attached at the side of it. It's Kantos construction."

She sucked in a breath. "Their base here on Crolla?"

"They'd need a base here, or bases. Somewhere to bring in the juvenile soldiers to the planet." He studied the bulbous outline. "There would also be a comms system."

"Something we could use to get a message out to the Eon." She smiled.

He nodded. "We can piggyback off the Kantos comms."

"But first, we need to get there and sneak in." She nodded. "We can do this, Thane."

He knew they could. He had the greatest motivation. Kaira might not want a mate, but he would protect her with his life.

"Let's get off this outcrop," he said.

She grabbed his arm and he felt her touch deeply.

"I'm sorry, Thane. I wish things could be different...for us."

There was true regret in her dark eyes.

He gave her a quick nod, despite his tight chest.

Just then, a faint buzzing sound filled the air.

He frowned. "Get down."

They lay flat against the rocks and Thane peered over the edge.

"Over there," she whispered, pointing to the left.

A small pack of Kantos soldiers came into view. They were moving fast, flowing across the rocky ground. Then they paused.

Thane noted they were a little thinner than the soldiers he usually encountered.

"Juveniles," she murmured.

They milled around a little and the one in the lead was looking toward the outcrop.

"You think they can detect us?" she asked.

"I don't think so. They might have been tracking the creatures that attacked us."

Finally, the juveniles moved away. The leader kept staring at the outcrop for a moment, before it finally swiveled and followed the others.

"Phew," Kaira said.

Thane watched until the soldiers disappeared into the haze. "Let's get going. It's a long journey to reach the Kantos base."

They climbed down, checking that the bear-wolves were gone, then headed in the direction of the Kantos base.

Thane's jaw was tight. It wouldn't be an easy journey. It was rough ground, and ahead lay another large patch of dense vegetation.

And who knew how many other predators and dangers they'd come across?

They moved into a light jog.

It was both torture and pleasure to be with his mate. A woman not interested in love or mating.

Surviving an aborted mating was difficult. It rarely ever happened. But once mated, he'd never heard of a rejection. He wasn't sure what would happen to him.

He couldn't worry about that now. He'd keep Kaira safe, and find a way off this Kantos planet.

He guessed his family really was cursed when it came to mating.

As they continued on, it got hotter, and both of them started sweating.

"The temperature's rising," Kaira said. "And the humidity."

The jungle patch was getting closer. It was far larger than the previous one.

Thane frowned. "Going around this will add substantial time. We'll need to go through it."

She straightened. "Let's do this."

Cautiously, they entered the jungle, stepping into the dappled shade. The trees were tall and twisted with vines. Neon-green sap leaked down the trunks.

Something moved in the dense vegetation, crashing away from them. They walked deeper, shoving vines out of the way.

He might need to form a sword to slash their way through. He shoved some bushes aside and saw a tiny, grass-covered clearing. He sensed life signs in the vegetation around them, but nothing too large. And the wildlife didn't seem interested in them, thankfully.

As they moved, he was excruciatingly conscious of Kaira beside him. The smell of her healthy sweat and her own scent teased his senses.

He gritted his teeth and kept moving.

Then he heard Kaira gasp.

He spun and saw her legs get pulled out from under her. She fell flat on her front.

"Kaira!"

"Something's attached to my leg."

Thane took two steps and spotted a long vine wrapped around her calf. He formed his sword.

Suddenly, she was yanked across the grass on her stomach. He heard her curse.

He ran after her. Another vine wrapped around her middle.

"Hold on, Kaira!"

Then something hit his back.

Suddenly, a vine wrapped around Thane. He fell and was dragged as well.

"Cren!"

He was yanked across the grass, right next to Kaira. Right in front of his eyes, several flowers bloomed along the length of the vines—small blooms in white and pink.

"I hate gardening." Kaira kicked, trying to get free. "I hate plants."

Thane tried to move his sword, but the vine was holding his arm tight.

A puff of pollen came from the flowers, hanging in the air around their heads. It smelled sickly sweet.

"What now?" Kaira muttered.

Thane's sword dissolved. His pulse spiked. He felt the bond between him and his helian go dull.

Like his helian was sleeping.

His armor started flowing away.

"Thane?" Kaira said. "My armor is disappearing."

"The pollen...it put my helian to sleep." He fought back a sharp spike of panic. He hoped to hell this was temporary.

Kaira coughed. "Whoa, my head is spinning."

"Kaira?"

"I'm all right, just whoozy."

Thane felt the faint effects of the pollen as well, like a muscle relaxant. "It must be the plant's defense mechanism. To stop us fighting it."

More vines wrapped around them, and then they were lifted upright, dangling there, caught in the vine's hold.

Thane's body collided with Kaira's. They were pressed firmly together as more vines wrapped them up tightly.

Her face pressed to his chest, just below his chin. Her breasts mashed against his chest.

Then they were yanked higher off the ground, up into the tree canopy.

"Oh, God," she said.

"Don't move."

"I *can't* move." She wriggled a bit.

He felt every movement she made. His muscles tightened.

The vines stopped. Thane and Kaira swung from the tree.

"Well, shit," she muttered.

He turned his head to the side. The ground was a long way down, but a fall shouldn't kill them. He hoped.

"Ideas?" she asked.

He tried again to command his helian. The bond wasn't broken, just sluggish.

"I can't connect properly with my helian." Frustration wound through him.

"Let me see if I can reach the vines. I can move one hand a bit." She moved her arm around him.

It pressed her harder against him and the feel of her made his cock stir. He ground his teeth together.

Cren. He needed to find some control.

"Almost..." She strained.

Thane felt her fingers brush his lower back.

"The vines are too tight, and they're damn strong." She slumped against him.

"We should conserve our strength. I'm hoping the effect of the pollen will wear off soon. Then I can use my helian again."

"Man, I feel like I had one too many margaritas."

"Margaritas?"

"Alcoholic drink. Delicious." She giggled.

He looked her down at her. It was such a sweet, unexpected sound. She tipped her head up and their faces were close.

"Damn, you're handsome, Thane."

He let out a breath. "Kaira."

"A sexy silver fox. How did you end up with hair so gray?"

"My grandfather and father were the same."

"I'm a blend of my mom and dad. Brown skin and eyes from my dad, and my height, or lack of it, from my mom."

Thane shifted a little and heard her gasp.

"Kaira? Did I hurt you?"

"No. Nope." Color streaked her cheeks.

He stilled. Her gaze locked with his and he saw it. *Desire.*

"Don't look at me like that," he said, voice deepening. "You said you couldn't do this."

"I know. I meant the mating thing." She licked her lips, her gaze settling on his mouth. "But that doesn't mean I'm not attracted."

He felt his gut knot with need. "Kaira, what the cren am I supposed to do with that?"

"I know." A husky whisper. "It's not fair to you." She shifted against him.

All his body felt was her, his mate. His unruly cock responded, and since it was jammed against her belly, she couldn't miss it.

Her eyes widened. "Thane."

"Ignore it. We're both under the effects of the pollen."

She swallowed. "It's pretty hard to ignore." Her chest was rising and falling quickly against his.

Pure torture.

"We need a distraction," she said. "Um…"

"What do you do in your time off?" he asked desperately.

"Time off?"

"Yes, when you aren't working."

She nibbled her lip and he made himself look away.

"I've been working a lot over the last year. Taking extra shifts. Keeping busy."

To deal with her grief. "There must be something you enjoy."

"Before…I loved to dance," she said quietly. "On my own. I enjoyed contemporary dance, just feeling the music." She sighed. "I haven't danced since my husband and father died."

He could see her being a dancer. She was graceful.

"What about you?" she asked.

"I like to read. I'm a huge fan of the renowned Eon poets, and classic stories about the great warriors."

She laughed. "I can totally see you sitting back, reading."

By Eschar's embrace, he liked this. Just being with her, talking together.

Then he felt a pulse of something.

"My helian's responding."

"Yes! Can you form your sword?"

"I think so."

"Okay, then we'd better get down before some creepy crawly decides we'd make a good snack."

Thane formed a knife. He shifted, their bodies rubbing together again. Ignoring the sensations, he got the knife on the vine and sawed. As soon as he cut into it, the vines all loosened suddenly.

"Shit!" Kaira yelped.

They both dropped and hit the verdant jungle floor.

"*Oof.*" Kaira rolled over, pushing up on one hand.

Thane rose to a crouch. "Are you all right?"

"Yes." She rose, dusting herself off.

Thane stood as well. "Then let's keep moving."

She gave a brisk nod and set off into the trees. They trudged through the undergrowth, the air hot and humid around them.

"Thane, look," Kaira breathed.

He glanced to the side, and through some vines covered in pretty yellow flowers, he saw ancient ruins nestled in the vegetation.

CHAPTER SIX

The ruins were made of black stone, and streaked with gray veins. There were some intact archways and pillars, but most were just crumbled ruins.

Kaira stepped onto the smooth, stone paving. The ruins were devoid of any growth or weeds. Strange patterns were inscribed on their surfaces.

"Incredible," Thane breathed.

"Some ancient species must have called this planet home." She stroked the stone archway. "It's so strange that it isn't covered in growth."

He frowned. "Very strange."

Kaira touched the archway again and stilled. "The stone's warm."

Suddenly, the ground vibrated under their feet. She spun, scanning for danger, and saw Thane do the same.

The archways trembled.

Kaira stumbled toward him. "What the hell?"

Then the archways moved and her pulse spiked.

The rocks moved, changing, transforming.

"Oh, my God," she breathed.

The stones shifted and lengthened, joining together until a huge, humanoid figure, made entirely of stone, almost as tall as the trees, towered over them.

Then it roared and slammed a giant stone fist into the ground.

The shockwave sent Kaira flying back into Thane.

"Uh-oh." She stared in horror as the creature, thing, whatever the hell it was, loomed over her and Thane.

The damn rocks had come to *life*.

"What is it?" she asked.

"I'm not sure. Its reading is organic. Perhaps some sort of silicon-based lifeform."

An alien made of rocks.

Thane formed a heavy axe, his fingers curling around the handle.

Kaira imagined a hammer, and it formed in her hands. Man, helians were incredible.

Thane rushed in and spun, slamming the axe against the alien's leg.

It cleaved into the rock, leaving a crack, but the creature stayed upright. It roared and swung a huge fist.

Thane ducked.

Kaira ran in behind the alien rock creature. With a cry, she swung her hammer and slammed it into the alien's back.

Several chips of rock flew off, but there was no real damage.

The creature spun and slammed its fists down on either side of her.

Crap.

"Kaira!"

Thane leaped onto the alien's arm. Kaira surged backward, and Thane smashed his axe down on the rock creature's elbow. A small chunk of rock fell off.

"Go," he yelled, leaping off.

She and Thane sprinted out of range.

"How the hell are we going to take it down?" she yelled.

"I'm not—"

The creature stomped on the ground, then waved a hand in front of its body.

Loose stones floated up in the air, hanging there.

Oh, shit. "Down!" She dived at Thane.

As they fell, the rocks flew at them like missiles. The pair of them hit the ground, the rocks flying overhead.

"Distract it," Thane said.

Kaira moved into a crouch. "What's your plan?"

He pushed up. "I'll let you know once I have one."

"Thane!" She didn't want him to get hurt.

He sprinted and circled around the alien.

"Hey." Kaira waved her arms. "Look here, stone man."

The creature's soulless stone face moved toward her. It took a lumbering step in her direction.

"That's it."

Suddenly, the creature moved. It was faster than she expected.

The stone giant swung an arm.

Kaira ducked. Its fist smashed into a tree, splintering the trunk.

She leaped back. *Yikes. Note to self: do not let the stone creature hit you.*

She ran, and the alien spun to keep her in sight. Loose, small rocks flew past her, and she dodged. One hit her back and she winced.

Thane attacked from behind with his axe.

The creature turned, grabbed the axe and yanked it out of Thane's hand.

Dammit. Kaira ran and jumped. She landed on the creature's arm.

Distracted, it spun again, and shook.

Kaira held on. Hell, it was like being on a bucking bull.

She lost her grip and flew off.

She smacked into the ground, the air knocked out of her. Her ears were ringing.

"Kaira, move!"

Thane's shout made her roll over.

The stone creature was stomping closer.

Oh, shit. She pushed up to move, but her boots slipped on some loose rocks.

"No!" Thane roared.

He ran at full speed, a newly formed axe in his hands.

The stone alien spun, its giant arms whirling.

A fist slammed into Thane, lifting him off his feet.

Kaira's heart stopped.

He flew through the air beyond the giant stone circle of the ruins, and crashed into a tree trunk. He dropped to the ground.

The creature focused on Kaira.

Crap. She needed to get to Thane. He wasn't moving.

Be okay, warrior. She fought back the tendrils of fear.

The stone alien stomped in her direction.

Kaira backed up. Her boots stepped off the stone floor and onto the grass.

The stone alien froze. It cocked its head, looking right through her.

Frowning, she stepped forward again, and as soon as her boot touched the stone, the alien stiffened and its attention zeroed back in on her.

Quickly, she backed off the stone and onto the grass again.

The creature paused, then turned and wandered to the center of the ruins, like it didn't have a care in the world.

As she watched, the rocks forming the creature fell apart, reforming the stone archway.

Her pulse jumped. The alien was somehow linked to the ruins.

She skirted the temple's stones, then ran toward Thane.

He was facedown in the rotting vegetation. She dropped to her knees beside him.

"Thane?"

No response.

She slid her arms under him and carefully tipped him over. With a shaking hand, she pressed her fingers to his neck. His pulse was strong, and it sent a small tremor of relief through her. He was alive.

"Thane?" She touched his face. He groaned and she saw he had a new bruise forming on his cheek.

She touched his stomach and he groaned again. She

probed. She didn't feel any broken ribs or anything that would indicate internal bleeding. But that didn't rule it out.

She touched his helian band and felt a jolt of warmth from it.

"Heal him," she whispered.

They couldn't stay here, exposed. She needed to find a spot for him to rest and recover.

She quickly scouted around, shoving at bushes and hoping she didn't come face-to-face with something poisonous or hungry.

Several huge trees speared into the sky. One had a large trunk, with a hole carved into the base, like a small cave.

Maybe created by some alien creature. She found a stick and poked around inside, cleaning out the dead, rotting leaves.

A small, spider-like creature skittered out.

She went back to the still-unconscious Thane and hooked her arms under his armpits.

"Okay, short trip, warrior."

She tugged and grunted, using her leg muscles. God, he was so heavy. Every inch of him was muscle.

Slowly, they inched across the ground and reached the tree.

With some more grunting and maneuvering, she got them inside the shelter of the tree.

She pulled out the water and dribbled some in his mouth. There wasn't much left.

"You're safe." She ran a hand over his hair. "Heal up, Thane. I need you."

THANE WOKE, feeling his helian's warmth and a sense of healing. He had no pain.

He instantly remembered the stone alien hitting him. There was a lot of pain then.

He shifted. His head was resting on Kaira's thigh. He smelled her, sensed her, like a piece of himself.

Quickly, he shut that down. She didn't want him, or what he had to offer.

"Thank God, you're awake. Are you all right?" she asked.

He blinked and looked around. It looked like they were in the hollow of a tree.

"Yes." He sat up, pressed a hand to his ribs.

It appeared everything was healing up nicely. He looked around. "You fought the alien, then dragged me in here?"

"You're really heavy, by the way."

He stared at her. Tough and incredible. These Terrans constantly amazed him. "Eon warriors have a dense muscle mass." He grabbed her hand. "Thank you."

She nodded. "I didn't have to fight the alien. It's linked to the ruins. Once I stepped off the stones, it lost interest and turned back into the architecture." She handed him the water. He noted that it was almost empty and took a small sip.

"So, we avoid any other ruins we see," he said.

"An excellent idea." Frowning, she rubbed her shoulder.

"You all right?"

"Just an itch. My armor repaired itself, at least. Are you ready to keep moving?"

"Yes."

Together they rose and stepped out of the tree. He heard the scuttling noises of small creatures in the bushes.

He hoped they were native animals, and not the Kantos.

They moved through the vegetation. Some snake-like reptiles dripped from the trees like hoses, but they mostly ignored them.

"This feels too easy." Kaira shoved a vine aside.

Thane agreed, his gut tight. He felt like something was coming. Something bad.

He shook his head and morphed his sword. "The vegetation is getting thicker." He slashed it apart for them.

Movement ahead. They both froze.

Small, furry, and nimble creatures ran up a tree, chittering and looking at them.

"Hey, little guys," Kaira called. "I visited my grandmother's hometown in India once. There were a whole bunch of monkeys at this temple I visited. They remind me of these guys. Cheeky."

One creature leaped onto Kaira. Thane tensed, but as the animal pulled on her hair and stuck a finger in her ear, she laughed.

He slowly relaxed. They appeared safe, and *by Eschar's embrace*, he loved the sound of her laugh.

"Look, the undergrowth is thinning out," she said.

Thane put his sword away and together they pushed through.

They'd reached the end of the jungle patch. The valley spread out before them. It was covered in knee-length grass, and nothing like the rocky terrain they'd left on the other side of the jungle. He looked at the mountain range in the distance.

The cocoon base was easier to spot now, looking like a cancerous growth.

"Keep an eye out for a water source," he said. "We need to replenish our supply."

"What are the odds it'll be drinkable?" she asked.

"There's always a chance."

They headed into the valley.

"You always an optimist?" she asked.

"As a doctor, I always hope I can heal my patients. I have to believe that."

"As head of security, I always think about worst-case scenarios." She shrugged. "And I've seen how life can snatch people away in the blink of an eye."

Thane's gut hardened. "You still grieve. For your husband and father."

"Grief never goes away; it just gets duller. Less acute." Her smile was sad. "Life goes on."

"And yet you won't let yourself love again."

She stiffened. "Some things aren't worth the risk." She glanced at him. "I'm sorry, I know mating is a big deal for you."

He nodded. "It's precious, but I understand your feelings, Kaira."

"You're a good man, Thane Kann-Eon."

He felt a stirring in his gut and looked away. He had to fight back the mating fever. If he'd been in Medical on the *Rengard*, he could probably formulate something to help.

He knew Kaira wouldn't feel the effects as strongly as he did. Those with a helian felt it first, and the most strongly, thanks to the symbiont amplifying the sensations. But as the mating fever grew, the effect would spill out onto her as well.

There was no way he'd accept her coming to him if it wasn't her choice. Driven by her baser needs.

"Look," Kaira said.

There was a quiet, fluttering sound. A huge flock of delicate, glowing insects with beautiful wings rose into the air. Thousands of them.

"Wow," she said. "They look like Earth butterflies."

The filmy pink wings glowed softly, and the small creatures danced around in the air.

Thane and Kaira walked on, the insects whirling and dancing above, the grass swishing around their ankles.

"Those must be their nests." Kaira nodded at the small mounds dotted across the valley. They were brown, and marked with streaks of the same pink as the butterflies on the sides.

They kept walking, and Thane's gut cramped. *Cren.* The mating fever was growing. He breathed deep and fought it back.

A faint vibration rumbled through the soles of his boots. "Do you feel that?

Kaira stilled. "Yeah."

One of the nearby butterfly nests burst open.

Another creature flew into the air. It was bulky, with a pyramid-shaped body that also glowed pink. Its wings flapped so fast they were a blur.

Below its body was a massive stinger.

Cren.

He grabbed Kaira. "Back up."

The insect made an annoyed buzzing noise.

"Is it Kantos?" she asked.

"Likely."

Another nest burst open on the left. A second, flying insect with a stinger rose into the air.

More nests opened.

"Kaira...run!"

They both sprinted down the valley.

The angry buzzing noise grew behind them.

Thane chanced a quick glance backward.

A flock of the stinger creatures were flying after them. The butterflies had scattered.

"They're coming!" he roared.

"There's nowhere to hide," Kaira yelled back.

The valley was long and wide. Full of nothing but grass.

Cren. Cren. Cren.

One creature darted forward, its stinger extended.

Thane spun and jabbed it with his sword. The creature darted to the side, and flew at him again.

He skewered it, and bright-pink fluid ran down his sword.

"Come on," Kaira yelled.

Together, they sprinted as fast as they could.

But the buzzing was growing, and several of the creatures swung around in front of them.

Thane and Kaira bumped into each other. The insects had formed a huge circle around them.

They had nowhere to go.

"Oh, fuck," she whispered.

"Just hold on."

She leaned into him, her gaze meeting his. "I don't want to die."

The insects buzzed closer.

Then all of a sudden, the ground crumbled away beneath them disappearing from under their feet.

"What the—?"

They both tumbled straight down, into the earth.

CHAPTER SEVEN

They crashed to the ground and rolled. Kaira groaned.

Thane leaned over her. "You okay?"

"Nothing's broken." At least, she was pretty sure nothing was broken.

She let him pull her up.

They were in a tunnel, and she looked up through the hole they'd fallen through. She could just see a patch of blue sky and that horrible buzzing sound was starting to grow louder.

"They're coming." Thane gripped her arm. "Let's go."

They ran down the tunnel. It looked naturally-formed to Kaira. The walls were banded with glowing and glittering strips of rocks and minerals. They maneuvered through a few gentle twists and turns.

They came to a junction. Several tunnels speared off in different directions. Cobwebs hung from the rocky ceiling, but they looked old and broken—not fresh.

Good. Hopefully, whatever made them was long gone.

"Are the bugs following us?" she asked.

"I'm not detecting them."

Her belly clenched. Why weren't they following?

Thane studied the tunnels. "I believe the Kantos base is in that direction."

They headed off into the tunnel to the left. More cobwebs decorated the walls and roof, and these ones were thicker, and looked newer.

"I don't like the look of those," she murmured.

Thane grunted.

They shoved through several of them and the filaments were sticky, clinging to her gloves. Then she spotted a large chamber ahead, that seemed to glow with a brighter light. They stepped closer, and she saw that there were holes up above, letting the light down.

A pool of still water sat in the center, a brilliant aqua color.

They moved closer, and Thane crouched and touched the water. She assumed he was using his helian to test it.

"The quality appears fine. It's drinkable." He filled up the bottle, and handed it to her. "The pool's deep. I can't sense the bottom."

She drank, detecting a faint sweet taste to the water. She handed the bottle back to him, then walked over to examine the walls. They were covered in moss. She touched it, and a blue color shimmered across it, leaving a bioluminescent glow on the tips of her gloves.

"Thane, the walls are really wet. There's moss growing on it."

He strode over to her. "Let's find a way out. There are more tunnels on the other side of the pool."

They skirted the water and tiredness tugged at her. She had no idea how much time had passed since their abduction, but the lack of sleep was starting to wear her down.

"You all right?" he asked.

She glanced up to see Thane watching her carefully.

She nodded. "Just tired. It's been a wild ride."

"I'll get you home. I promise."

"*We'll* get home," she said.

There was an intense look in his black-green eyes, and he nodded.

Several tunnel entrances peppered the wall ahead of them.

"I think the right-hand one is best—" He broke off with a groan, going down on one knee.

Her pulse jumped. "Thane?" She crouched beside him. "What's wrong?" She pressed a hand to his back. *God, was he hurt?*

"Don't touch me." He shifted away from her.

She felt a strange punch to her gut, and dropped her hand.

He was breathing heavily, his body shaking.

Screw this. She moved around in front of him and crouched. "Let me help you."

His head lifted. The green in his eyes looked alive. "I'm feeling stirrings of the Eon mating fever."

"*Oh.*" Her belly was alive with flutters.

"I won't hurt you. I...just need a minute to get it under control."

"The mating fever...?"

"It makes me want to touch you." His body shuddered.

She dragged in a deep breath. She stared at him. He was a good man. An honorable man. He'd protected her, been with her every step of this horrible situation.

She cupped his cheeks.

"Kaira—"

She kissed him.

He groaned and she deepened the kiss, pulling in the taste of him. She kept it slow. Desire was a slow simmer in her belly.

She might not want to be mated, but she wanted him.

He shuddered, but didn't touch her. Except his mouth moved on hers—firm, demanding. So, so good.

Kaira forced herself to pull back.

They stared at each other for a beat. He looked better, and his breathing had evened out.

"Come on." She helped him up.

"I'm good. Thank you." He looked to the tunnels, gathering himself. "Let's get going. I want to find a way out of this underground maze."

Small rocks crunched under their boots.

"The quicker we get out of here and get to the Kantos base, the better," he said.

"You think the Eon are looking for us?" she asked.

"Yes, and when they get our signal, they'll be here as fast as they can."

Good. Kaira wanted off this planet.

A rumble echoed through the tunnel.

They both froze.

The ground and walls started to shake, and dust rained down on them.

"What now?" she said.

Thane turned, looking back the way they'd come.

"What is it?" she asked.

"I hear water."

He strode back down the tunnel, and Kaira jogged to follow. They turned a bend, and ahead, she could see the chamber and the pool they'd left behind.

Her heart stopped. "Oh, God."

The water in the pool was rising up, starting to flood through the chamber.

Thane spun. "Run."

"It's not so bad—"

"It's rising faster."

He took her hand and they ran. It wasn't long before her chest was burning. Kaira stumbled, but Thane caught her.

She heard the rush of water coming behind them with a loud roar. *Shit*. There was no way they'd be able to outrun it.

Thane stopped and pulled her close.

"We can't beat it," he said.

Her heart thumped hard against her ribs.

"Hold on." He wrapped himself around her. His armor changed, the black scales twining around them both like a rope. He'd tied them together.

"Thane." Fear drummed through her.

"I'm here." His gaze met hers.

Then a wall of water rushed down the tunnel toward them.

Oh, God.

She bit her lip and held onto him tighter.

Then the water hit them and swept them away.

THANE HELD on tight to Kaira. They were swept along, tumbling over and over.

He sucked in a breath, and heard Kaira spluttering.

He kicked his legs, trying to keep their heads above the deluge. He knew he could form helmets, but one big knock against a rock could shatter it in their faces.

A deafening roar reached his ears, and he realized in a flash what was ahead. He thrust a hand out.

He caught a rock and stopped their mad rush.

They'd reached the top of a huge fall of water. The tunnel opened into a large chasm below.

"Shit!" Kaira yelled.

Thane gripped the rock harder, trying to hold on.

They were hanging over the drop, water rushing over them.

"Can't...hold on much longer." Every muscle in his arm strained.

Kaira touched his face. "Let go."

"No. Have to...keep you safe."

But his fingers were slipping.

"I'll release the armor, and you climb up."

"Hell no, warrior. Let go. We'll fall together."

His gut clenched. "Kaira—"

Her face was resolute. "Do it."

He let go.

The water washed them over the edge.

As they fell, he curled his body around hers. He spun so he was on the bottom.

A second later, they hit a pool with a huge splash.

Bubbles rose around him and Thane kicked. Finally, their heads broke the surface.

Kaira spluttered. "I always hated waterslides as a kid."

Holding her tight, Thane kicked to the side.

It was another pool of water, being filled by the roaring flow tumbling down from above. He reached the edge and dragged them both onto the rocky shore.

Kaira flopped on her back. Her wet hair stuck to her head.

As they watched, the waterfall slowly decreased, and then stopped.

She grabbed his hand and squeezed.

He squeezed back.

"We need to search for a way out." He didn't want to be here if the water started rising again.

She nodded and pushed to her feet. Then she swayed.

"Kaira?"

He swung her around. She blinked, her eyes unfocused.

"I... It hurts."

"What?" he demanded.

Her cheeks were flushed. He touched her neck. She was burning up.

"Kaira, tell me—"

She collapsed.

Thane caught her and lifted her into his arms. He moved away from the water's edge and set her down on the stone floor.

She moaned.

"Hold on, Kaira." He touched her face.

Her eyes were completely unfocused, like she didn't see him.

Panic was slick in his veins, and Thane fought to find the doctor inside him. He'd treated thousands of people without ever letting fear take over.

But this time, he couldn't quite find that calm. He commanded his helian, and her scale armor melted away. Instantly, he saw her shirt was torn. When he saw her shoulder, he hissed.

It was red and inflamed where she'd been scratched.

He cursed.

"Thane." Her voice was weak and she thrashed.

"Shh. I'm going to take care of you."

"Hurts."

He studied the scratch. It was infected. Likely some sort of poison.

He needed to use *havv,* and he only had one vial with him. He hadn't been expecting to be abducted when he'd visited Earth. He pulled it out without hesitation and dripped it onto her wound. He smoothed it over her skin.

She writhed.

"I know. I know." He pulled her into his lap. "Let the healing happen."

There was sweat on her brow, and her eyes opened. Her pupils were dilated.

"Thane?"

"I'm here."

Her brow creased and her gaze latched onto his face.

"You're really pretty," she murmured.

He fought back a smile. "Just rest now."

"I love your eyes. And your jaw. And your lips." She made a sound. "I really like kissing you."

He fought back a groan.

"I want you so badly, but I'm so afraid to reach out."

"Kaira—" His hands flexed on her. She was killing him.

"Could fall for you," she whispered. "Strong, smart, sexy warrior."

"Kaira." He pressed his forehead to hers. "You'll hate that you told me this."

"Glad we're together. Whatever happens, I'm really glad you're with me, Thane."

"Me too, Starlight. Now rest."

"Starlight. Like that."

"It's from a famous Eon poem. A warrior calls his most cherished mate his starlight in the darkness."

"Pretty." Her eyelashes fluttered closed. She had thick, ridiculously long lashes.

Thane sat back and stroked her temple.

His mate was beautiful. With her brown skin, high cheekbones and those long eyelashes. And so small, yet so strong and tough. A mix of contradictions, his mate.

Telling him that she would never get close to someone again, then telling him that she wanted him.

Cren.

He wanted her so much he could barely breathe.

He stroked her dark hair. It was drying after their trip through the water. All he could focus on was getting to the Kantos base, getting the message out, and keeping Kaira safe.

Until they made it off Crolla, he wouldn't risk her by giving into his desire.

Then he felt the stirring of the mating fever.

He gritted his teeth. He *would* protect her, from himself, as well.

"Rest now, Kaira."

He stayed close, watching the rise and fall of her chest. She seemed to be resting calmly now.

He needed her healed so they could keep moving and get to the base.

For now, he'd keep watch and make sure nothing disturbed her sleep.

CHAPTER EIGHT

S he blinked her eyes. She felt like she'd been run over by a truck.

"Kaira?"

Thane's handsome face came into view. God, she could stare at him all day.

"You with me?" he asked.

She nodded. "What happened? I remember the waterfall from hell, then it gets hazy."

"You were scratched by those bear predators. It was poisoning you."

She touched her shoulder, remembering burning pain. "It feels okay now. I'm just tired."

"The *havv* fixed the injury, and my helian will do what it can to feed you some energy."

Because they were mates. For some reason, the thought didn't make her panic quite so much.

Kaira sat up and nearly fell sideways.

Thane grabbed her and pulled her against his chest. "Easy."

She might need another minute or two. "We need to find a way out—"

"Rest. Doctor's orders."

With a sigh, she leaned against him. He was so warm. She moved her hand and it landed on his thigh.

They both stiffened. She lifted her hand.

"Don't," he said. "Don't move it."

She hesitated, then let her hand drop to his corded thigh.

It felt good.

"Tell me about being a doctor. Do you like it?" Not the smoothest change of subject.

"Yes. It's my calling. I like healing people. I like solving challenges."

And he was an excellent warrior. She'd seen him fight. He was good.

"Do you like the Air Force?" he asked.

She nodded. "I like the order, and the challenges, and serving my country." She resisted the urge to stroke the muscles under her fingers. "Although, I realize I've been all work since..."

"You lost your husband."

She nodded. "This experience is a good reminder that I need to live a little more."

His hand moved to the back of her neck and squeezed. A quiet understanding. She closed her eyes. She was so drawn to him.

They sat in companionable silence. Together they watched the pool of water, so still and calm.

"I'm going to look around." He shifted and rose. "You keep resting."

"I can—"

He raised a brow. "Doctor's orders."

She rolled her eyes. "Does that really work for you?"

"Most of the time."

She watched him circle the pool and check the walls. He crouched, touching some of the rocks.

Her gaze moved down his body. She loved the easy way he moved his powerful form.

He finally wandered back her way and she pushed to her feet. She was feeling better, steadier.

"There are some shafts in the far wall," he said.

"But?" She heard it in his voice.

"But they go down. There's no other way out of here, except the way we came in."

Kaira glanced at the cliff they'd fallen down. The sheer walls didn't look scalable. "Well, maybe if we go down, we'll find a way up." A yawn hit her.

He eyed her. "We should find somewhere to rest, get some sleep."

"I vote we go down."

He nodded. "We'll have to climb."

She lifted her chin. "I'm ready."

They circled the pool. Thankfully, there were no signs of any more floods.

They reached the wall, and she spotted the holes he was talking about. Thane waved her in.

Kaira poked her head in and turned to look downward. The rock walls were rough, and the shaft was roughly circular, like a chimney. It had a slight slant to it, which would help with the climb.

"I'll go first," Thane said.

She watched him climb into the shaft and start inching down.

Right. She pressed a boot to the wall and climbed out over the hole.

Ugh. This wasn't going to be easy.

She moved downward, moving her hands and feet, one after the other.

God, if they slipped...

Kaira gritted her teeth. She just had to think about getting out of here, then into the Kantos base.

Suddenly, her hand slipped, and she lost her grip.

Shit.

She dropped and smacked into Thane.

Thankfully, they didn't fall. He'd locked his arms and legs, and was holding them still.

"Jesus. Sorry."

"You all right?" he rumbled in her ear.

She nodded and reached for the wall, conscious that she was plastered against his body.

She got a grip and steadied herself. They kept moving.

"We're close to the bottom," he said.

A second later, she moved out of the shaft behind him.

She stepped out into a cavern awash in a blue-white glow.

"Oh my..."

It looked like a fairytale. Bioluminescent plants covered the walls. Some dripped down from the ceiling, looking like strands of fairy lights. There was another small pool of water in the center of the space, with the same blue glow as the plants.

"It's beautiful," she said.

"Kaira, look." Thane walked toward the far wall.

She gasped. The stone wall was covered in symbols. There were circles and lines, all painted in a glimmering gold. They linked together in intricate designs.

"Some sort of language?" She touched a line and a pulse of light flared across the concentric circles.

"These might belong to whatever ancient culture lived on Crolla before the Kantos came," Thane said.

"Maybe the same aliens who built the stone ruins above." Sadness washed through her. No doubt they'd been victims of the Kantos as well.

There was a sound behind them. The crunch of rocks under a foot.

They both spun.

She didn't see anything in the cavern.

Both of them tensed and scanned around.

"Anything?" she asked.

"I'm not picking up any life signs."

"Okay, well I suggest we rest." She yawned again. Tiredness was dragging on her like a heavy blanket. "I—"

There was a sudden burst of bright light. She blinked and several figures appeared out of nowhere.

"Thane!" She threw up an arm.

Something hit her on the back of her legs and she dropped to her knees. When she looked up, spears were pointed at her head. She heard Thane grunt.

The light returned to normal and she saw several muscled warriors around her. They all had ghost-white, pearlescent skin with a faint blue undertone. They all wore fitted, gray trousers, and had bare chests. They were lean, with muscled abs and strong arms. She looked up.

They had no hair, just smooth heads and eyes that were pure white. She glanced over and noted several more warriors surrounding Thane. He was on his knees as well, his hands in the air. One of the warriors had a spear pointed right to his lower back.

"Who are you?" she asked.

One warrior turned his head in her direction. He had a carved jaw, high cheekbones, but a sightless gaze that seemed to look right through her.

He said something in a deep, resonant voice, but she didn't understand the musical language.

"He said they are the Mollai," Thane translated.

Of course, Thane understood. He'd have lingual tech implanted, like Space Corps officers did.

The warrior's skin glowed and he looked at another warrior. Kaira realized that the second warrior was a woman. She was shirtless like the others, but with small, high breasts. She looked like a marble statue.

Kaira realized they were communicating. "They're telepathic?"

Thane nodded.

The warrior stepped closer and said something. Grumbles filled the cavern from the other warriors.

"He asked if we're with the ravagers," Thane said. "He must mean the Kantos." Thane spoke back in the same musical language.

The warrior studied Thane, then Kaira. He spoke again.

Thane's brows drew together. "He said, if you allow him, he can use his telepathy to help you understand their language."

Kaira swallowed. She didn't like the idea of anyone having access to her brain, but at least he'd asked her permission. "Do you think we can trust them?"

"They consider the Kantos their enemy, so I think so."

She traded a glance with Thane, then she nodded.

The warrior didn't touch her, but she felt the faintest warmth encircle her skull.

Here goes nothing. "You're native to Crolla?"

"Yes," the warrior replied. "This is our planet, and has been since the birth of the Mollai."

Oh, wow. She understood every word he said. He was facing her, but his white eyes didn't seem focused on her. She lifted a hand and waved it a little.

"I am not blind, intruder, although we do not rely solely on our vision alone."

"Right. Sorry. So you're enemies of the Kantos?"

"Yes. The invaders. The ravagers." Anger vibrated in the warrior's voice.

"We aren't with them," Kaira said. "They are our enemy, too. They're planning to invade my planet." She gestured at Thane. "Thane's people are helping us fight them."

The warrior stared at her. She guessed his vision wasn't that great, but she didn't doubt he had other acute senses.

"Why are you here?" he asked.

"The Kantos took us," Thane said. "They dumped us here for their young soldiers to hunt."

The warrior scowled. "Bands of the young invaders roam the planet. Killing, consuming."

"We aren't lying," Kaira said. "The Kantos are our enemy as well."

The warrior was silent for a moment, then nodded his head. "Come. We'll take you to meet Aurelai."

"Who's that?" Slowly, Kaira rose, and moved over to Thane. He took her hand.

"She is our leader," the warrior said. "Now, walk, intruders."

THE MOLLAI WARRIORS led Thane and Kaira through twisting tunnels. The place was a maze, and he knew they would never find a way out on their own.

"This is a good defense," Kaira said. "If the Kantos ever got in here, there's no way they could navigate this."

The lead warrior stopped in front of a stone wall. It was covered with more of the geometric gold markings they'd seen before.

He stepped forward and pressed his hand to the stone.

A glow pulsed through the markings, then the stone groaned, and a portion of the wall slid open.

"Come." He waved them inside.

Thane sensed that the warriors were still tense and alert. The leader didn't trust them.

They moved down another tunnel and it slowly widened.

The art in here was different. There were images of pale blue-white Mollai figures dancing, sharing meals, farming what looked like beautiful, white flowers. Some of the art was more erotic—couples entwined together in intimate embraces. A man and a woman holding each other, two women kissing, others with two, three and even four males making love.

They stepped into a large, domed cavern, and Thane knew they were deep underground, but it was washed in white-blue light.

Bioluminescent plants covered the ceiling. The space was dotted with carved stone furniture and large, white pillows.

The warriors marched them to the center of the cavern. Other pale-skinned Mollai watched, both adults and children. One child watched them pass, holding a small frog-like creature clutched in his small hands.

All the Mollai wore gray pants, with their torsos bare. Some wore tight trousers like the warriors, others had looser, flowing garments.

"What have we here?"

A woman stepped forward. She was young with a slender body and a long neck. An intricate gold necklace wound around her neck, and her breasts were high and full.

"Aurelai, we found these two in the caves. They said they are enemies of the ravagers."

"Really?" The woman's sightless eyes focused on them.

"We were abducted by the Kantos from my planet," Kaira said. "We're trying to find a way to contact Thane's people and avoid the planet's predators until we can be rescued."

The woman turned. "Lennar, you've been gruff and rude to these poor people. They need our help."

The lead warrior scowled. "Your safety, and the safety of our people, is my first priority. Not the comfort of strangers who invade our tunnels."

"He's right." Thane agreed with the warrior. "He's done nothing except what I expect of a warrior protecting his people."

"Men." The Mollai woman stepped forward. "I am Aurelai, leader of the Mollai." She held out a slender hand. "Welcome."

"I'm Kaira. Kaira Chand of Earth." Kaira touched the woman's hand—brown skin against white. "And this is Thane Kann-Eon of the Eon Empire."

"You are both welcome. Come." The woman led them deeper into the cavern. "You must be tired and hungry."

"It's been a pretty wild trip," Kaira said. "Your planet is dangerous."

"The above has been contaminated by the ravagers. The Kantos. They brought dangerous creatures here to breed and hunt."

"We saw ruins," Thane said. "Do they belong to your people?"

A sad look crossed Aurelai's regal face. "No. The Mollai have always been a people of the below. But our cousins, the Tollai, once called the above home."

"There weren't many Tollai left," Lennar said. "Then the Kantos wiped them out."

Aurelai waved at some large, white pillows on the floor. Kaira and Thane sat.

"We moved deeper to avoid the Kantos," the Mollai leader told them.

"And we have our defenses," Lennar added.

"We fell into the tunnels," Thane said. "The Kantos were chasing us, but they didn't follow us down here."

"Then we got washed away by a flood of water," Kaira said.

Aurelai gasped. "Lennar!"

"We didn't know who they were." The warrior shifted uneasily.

"The water is one of our defenses," Aurelai said. "I'm very glad you weren't hurt." She looked up, and waved a hand.

Some men and women brought over platters filled with glowing, white flowers and set them down. They looked like the ones they'd seen in the artwork. There were also urns and glasses of pale-blue liquid.

"Please eat," Aurelai said. "You're safe here."

Thane checked the food and drink, and his helian pulsed. He nodded at Kaira.

He took a long drink of the blue fluid. It was sweet and refreshing. He watched the Mollai eat the flowers, and gingerly bit into one of the petals. They were thick and fleshy, and had a unique flavor.

"These taste like chicken," Kaira said, chewing on a flower.

"We grow the *neelianna* down here. It provides all we need."

The Mollai in the cavern started to relax. Conversation resumed.

"Would you like to wash and change?" Aurelai asked.

Kaira nodded. "Please."

She was led away by the women. Lennar led Thane to a different side room. Inside, he saw a natural basin of rock filled with water that dripped down the walls.

"There are fresh clothes on the bench," the warrior said.

There was a stone bench cut into the far wall. A stack of neatly folded gray clothes rested on it.

"Thank you, Lennar. We don't mean your people any harm. We need to find a way to the surface. We plan to find a way to the Kantos base, so we can get a message to my ship."

"Ship?"

"My people are warriors. We travel the stars."

A look crossed Lennar's face. "Incredible." The warrior shook his head. "Our home is deep in the below, but I've seen the night sky a few times. It looks like our caverns filled with *gala* worms. Beautiful." Lennar backed out. "Wash. Change. We'll talk more after."

Thane retracted his armor, then splashed his face and body with water. His uniform smelled of sweat and he shucked it off. He pulled on some gray pants like the other warriors wore. There were no shirts in the pile of clothes, so he'd have to go shirtless like the Mollai.

Finally, he walked out of the room and stopped.

He saw Kaira smiling as she walked out of another

room. She wore loose gray pants, and just a black sports top that she'd clearly been wearing under her clothes. It cupped her breasts tightly and left her flat, toned belly bare.

Her gaze met his.

"It's nice to freshen up," she said.

He nodded. They walked together to rejoin Aurelai. The protective Lennar hovered near the Mollai leader.

They ate more flowers. Drank. More Mollai brought bowls of jellied flowers that Aurelai told them was a dessert.

"So, you avoid the Kantos?" Thane asked.

Lennar nodded. "We surveil them, but they don't often venture down here." A faint smile. "They've learned not to."

Kaira leaned forward. "You don't want to fight the Kantos? Drive them off your planet?"

Aurelai shook her head. "Our numbers are not great, and many of our population are only children. We have warriors for protection, but we aren't fighters. We live, love, create, celebrate. We don't have it in us to destroy our lives to fight a war."

Thane didn't think Lennar agreed, but the warrior did nod. "We cannot match the numbers of the ravagers."

"Please eat, drink, and recharge," Aurelai said. "We offer you sanctuary for as long as you need it."

"Thank you, Aurelai." Thane met Lennar's gaze. "Tomorrow, we need a way to the surface."

"We have to contact our people," Kaira said.

Aurelai nodded. "I understand. Lennar will show you to the above tomorrow, but for now, rest."

The Mollai leader clapped her hands.

Music started. People played delicate stringed instruments and tiny flutes.

Kaira shifted on the cushion, her shoulder brushing against Thane's. He sensed that his mate was relaxed and happy.

He finally let himself relax.

This would be a much-needed pause before they faced the Kantos again.

CHAPTER NINE

K aira tapped a toe to the music. It had a haunting undertone, but a sweet, romantic beat.

Her belly was full. She couldn't believe how filling the *neelianna* flowers were. She'd also had two bowls of the Mollai dessert.

She was tired, but she was relaxed. For a moment, she could let the stress of this ordeal melt away. Take a short break to recharge.

She and Thane were alive. That's what mattered.

She glanced sideways at him as he watched the musicians. His bare chest was a huge distraction. He had slabs of toned muscle that she wanted to stare at. Her fingers itched to touch. A doctor should not be built like that.

Some Mollai got up to dance. The younger children joined in with excited squeals, moving with great abandon and enthusiasm. All the older couples moved slower, gracefully in sync with the music.

Smiling, she watched as a man whirled a smiling woman into his arms.

"Music is an important part of our culture." Aurelai said. "Our vision is not as acute as yours, as it's not needed down here. But we possess very good hearing, so music resonates with us deeply. And we love art and gardening. Creation."

Some girls came over to Aurelai. With a smile, the Mollai leader let them take her onto the dance floor. Then the woman dipped and swirled as she danced.

"She's good," Kaira said.

"Very graceful," Thane agreed.

Lennar stomped over to the leader, a scowl on his face.

Aurelai cupped the man's cheek, smiled, then kissed the warrior.

Oh, they were a couple. The pair moved into a close dance, moving as one. Lennar was a good dancer, too. He held Aurelai tucked closely against him.

"Can you dance?" Kaira asked Thane.

"No. That's not part of an Eon warrior's training."

More children raced over. They shyly touched Kaira's dark hair, entranced. Then they pulled her to her feet.

Thane smiled. "Go."

She let herself be dragged onto the dance floor.

She moved to the music and smiled at the children. Then she closed her eyes. Her body turned languid, like water. She lifted her arms, then bent backward and flowed.

It had been so long since she'd danced. She'd always loved losing herself to the rhythm. The music changed, and she felt it in her veins. She moved, turned, dipped.

She opened her eyes. Many of the Mollai were watching her with appreciation.

She turned.

Thane was watching her too.

Her chest locked, heat curling in her belly.

The look in his eyes...

She kept moving, dancing just for him. Joy, desire, heat, it all coalesced inside her. She spun and looked back.

Thane's green-black eyes were on her. The blue-white light of the cavern didn't diminish the gold of his skin, the handsome lines of his face. There was such heat in the way he watched her.

Desire arrowed through her, and pulsed between her legs.

She wanted this man so much, but it wasn't fair to take things any further between them, not when it would mean far more to him.

Some young women whirled around her. She looked back, and Thane was gone.

When the song ended, Kaira finished dancing. Aurelai appeared, holding two glasses in her hand. She handed one to Kaira.

"You dance well, Kaira."

"Thank you." She sipped her drink. "It's been a long time." And it felt good. She'd missed it. She looked around. *Where had Thane gone?*

Aurelai smiled. "Your man is in the room over there." She pointed. "He asked for a private space. Sleep well, Kaira of Earth."

Kaira headed toward the room and noted two women

hovering in the doorway, peering in. She saw interest on their faces. When she looked through the doorway, she saw Thane, still shirtless, moving through some sort of routine. He lunged, and thrust his arms forward. It looked like a warrior version of tai chi.

The female Mollai watched him intently, and one licked her lips.

Kaira felt a twist inside her. She glared at them.

One elbowed the other, and they withdrew.

She entered and closed the door behind her. She continued to watch Thane move, admiring the entrancing flex of his strong muscles.

Finally, he stopped and turned to her. "Finished dancing?"

"Yes, I won't lie, it felt good, but I'm asleep on my feet."

"We both need sleep. Tomorrow, Lennar will take us to the surface." Thane's face turned serious. "Then we need to find a way into the Kantos base."

She nodded. "What were you doing before?"

"*Dura*. An ancient form of meditation and training. A way to center a warrior's mind and body."

"You're easy to watch."

"Like watching you dance. You looked like starlight on water."

She felt heat in her cheeks and felt so confused by the wild mix of emotions inside her.

"I'd better find my room." She forced the words out, even though she was reluctant to leave.

Thane grabbed her arm. "Stay. We both need sleep.

The Mollai have been nothing but kind, but I'd prefer you close."

She wasn't sure that was a good idea, but she couldn't say no.

They settled on the large sleeping cushion. It had a silky-smooth cover and as soon as they lay down, the glow of the plants around them automatically dimmed.

Thane lay flat on his back beside her and pulled the thin sheet over them both.

"Good night, Thane."

"Rest well, Kaira."

She thought she wouldn't be able to sleep, but she drifted off, knowing that Thane was right beside her.

She woke at some point, her heart in her throat, not sure where she was.

Then she felt the large body wrapped around her. Thane was pressed against her back, one strong arm tucked under her breasts, one heavy leg pinning hers. The warmth of him engulfed her.

Safe.

She snuggled deeper into his hard body and fell back to sleep.

When she woke again, she felt Thane moving restlessly. He was really hot. He groaned and she opened her eyes. She saw golden skin right in front of her and realized she was pressed to his front, her face nestled into his neck.

Something was wrong with him. He was still asleep, but heat was pumping off his body and he was unsettled.

Then she felt the hard erection against her thigh.

Oh. God.

He groaned again like he was in pain. His skin was covered in a light sheen of sweat.

Was this the mating fever?

Kaira shifted and his arms tightened on her. Desire pulsed in her belly. She bit her lip and stroked her hand down his chest. She wanted to touch, soothe...

"Kaira."

She glanced up, but he wasn't awake. His eyes were still closed. He moved against her, shifting their bodies until his cock rested against her belly.

She bit back a moan. She didn't let herself think, she just followed the instincts inside her.

She reached down and stroked the bulge in his gray pants.

Another masculine groan, and he pushed into her hand.

Oh, boy. She squeezed him.

Another harsh sound, and his hips pumped forward. Then his body tensed. "Kaira?"

She looked up. He was awake now, his brow creased.

"Cren, I'm sorry, I—"

"Don't be." Her voice was husky. "Thane, can I touch you?"

He inhaled harshly. "Yes. No. *Wait.*" His body shuddered. "Only if you want to... *Cren.*"

"I want to." She pushed his trousers down and his cock bounced free. She circled the thick length with her hand.

He gave a long groan. "*Kaira.*"

His erection was huge. Desire licked her insides and

she stroked him harder, her fingers running over the veined head.

Thane made a low, guttural sound. His face twisted. "Faster, Starlight."

Kaira pumped his cock faster.

"I've never been this hard," he growled.

She pressed her lips to his neck and never slowed her strokes of that big, thick cock. She wanted it inside her. Filling up the emptiness gnawing at her. Joining them together.

He let out a tortured groan.

"Come, Thane." She bit him hard, the tendon in his neck between her teeth.

A strangled sound broke free of him, then wetness spurted over her hands and belly.

She pressed into him, both of them panting.

This was the sexiest thing she'd shared with anyone in a long time.

"Kaira..."

"Don't say anything," she said.

His arms tightened on her. They were silent for a while as their breathing returned to normal.

"We should clean up, and get our armor on." There was reluctance in his voice. "We need to go soon."

She sighed. A part of her screamed at her to back away from him, to keep her distance. But she just couldn't anymore.

None of that mattered anyway. Their little respite was over.

It was time to get back to reality.

KAIRA FOLLOWED Thane and Lennar through the tunnels.

She tried to focus on the mission ahead, but she was very aware of Thane walking just ahead of her.

Touching him, stroking that generous cock... She fought back a shudder. She'd loved every minute of touching him.

Can't think of this now, Chand. She gritted her teeth. They were headed to the surface and she needed to focus on that.

"Here." Lennar stopped. The warrior touched the gold etchings on the wall.

Rock retracted to show a small, circular chamber beyond. The faint whistle of air filled the space around them.

"This will carry you to the surface." Lennar inclined his head. "It has been an honor to meet you both."

"Thank you, Lennar," Thane said. "The assistance of the Mollai has helped us greatly."

"We really appreciate your help." Kaira smiled.

"Good luck, Kaira and Thane. I hope you find your people, and can defeat the Kantos."

"I'll go first," Thane said.

He reached the entrance to the chamber and leaned in.

The rush of air sounded strong, even from where Kaira stood. Thane nodded to Lennar and his warriors, then looked at her.

"See you at the top." He stepped inside.

He was whooshed upward fast and was gone.

Kaira nodded at Lennar, then stepped into the shaft.

She shot upward, the air rushing past her. Then she flew out of the shaft and into the morning sunlight. She landed in a crouch on the rocky surface.

"Are you all right?" Thane was right beside her.

"Ooh, that was a fun ride." She straightened and looked around.

The mountains were closer, looming up into the sky.

She could see the cocoon base clearly now. Her belly tightened. There were also dozens of flying bugs moving in and out of it.

How the hell were they going to get up there?

"Look." Thane tapped her shoulder. In the distance, a road wound its way up the side of the mountain. There was a steep drop on one side, rock walls on the other.

"Let's check it out," she said.

They broke into a jog. The rocky hill gave way to a flatter grassland.

They reached a patch of flattened grass. A half-mauled animal lay on its side. Its side was torn up and bloody. Lots of clawed footprints covered the ground around it.

Kaira frowned. Then a clicking buzz filled the air.

"Soldiers," Thane hissed.

Shit. "Into the grass."

They dived into a long patch of grass. Tense, they waited.

The buzzing got louder.

A small group of juvenile soldiers appeared. They hurried toward the carcass and started tearing into it.

Kaira pushed some blades of grass aside, watching the feeding frenzy. She grimaced.

One of the soldiers lifted its head. And looked their way.

Crap. She froze and felt Thane tense too.

The soldier took a step toward them.

No. Go away. She willed the damn alien to look the other way.

Suddenly, another soldier butted into the one watching them. It buzzed angrily and the two soldiers slapped at each other.

The group of juveniles kept eating until the dead animal was just a skeleton. Kaira's muscles were aching from holding still so long.

Finally, the group moved away.

That's it. One paused to look back, and Kaira couldn't tell if it was the same one as before. Just as her pulse tripped, it dashed away after the others and was gone.

Thane released a breath. "That was close."

"Let's get out of here," she said.

They kept low in the grass as they jogged toward the road. There was no sign of the group of juveniles.

Suddenly, the roar of a large animal sounded nearby.

They ducked down into the grass again. Next, there was an odd rattling sound.

A moment later, a huge beast—it looked like a mammoth, its large body covered in shaggy, gray fur—appeared, pulling a long, black cart behind it.

A hunched Kantos soldier sat in front of the cart, directing the beast.

The cart slowed, and then started up the winding road.

"Come on," she whispered.

They kept low and stayed out of sight, following behind. The cart rounded a corner, and they ducked down behind some large, black boulders.

Oh, crap.

Ahead, the cart passed through a rock structure with an archway cut through the center of it. It was some sort of gatehouse. Kantos soldiers were everywhere. Her heart kicked in her chest.

"You see any way past the guard house?" she asked.

Grim faced, Thane shook his head.

Dammit. There was no way through.

A bug appeared farther down on the path. It was about the size of a dog, a mottled black-brown, with long antennae. It lifted its head, sniffing the air, and its gaze turned in their direction.

Oh, shit.

"We have to go." Thane pulled her back.

They ran back down the path. At the base of the mountains, the ground was littered with huge, broken rocks.

"Right." She rested her hands on her hips. "We need to—"

All of a sudden, Thane groaned and doubled over.

"Thane," she gasped.

He pressed his hand to his flat stomach, and held his other one up.

"What's wrong?" she demanded. "Is it the mating fever?"

———

THANE DRAGGED IN A BREATH, and fought back the cramps wracking through him.

He scented Kaira, felt her warmth, heard her quick breaths. Desire was like a fist in his gut.

He had to fight this back. For her.

"Thane?" She touched a hand to his shoulder.

He closed his eyes and pulled strength from her touch.

He straightened. "I'm fine."

"You're *not* fine." Concern lined her face.

"No. Come on, we need to—" With a groan, he went down on one knee.

"Thane." She knelt. "Talk to me, damn you."

He met her gaze. *By Eschar's embrace*, she was so beautiful. Desire roared higher inside him.

"It is the mating fever."

She sat back. "Tell me more about it." Her face hardened. "Don't lie to me."

"It happens between mates to cement the bond."

She frowned. "This'll get worse?"

He nodded. "If I was on my warship, I might be able to suppress it."

"It makes you want to—" She licked her lips.

He zeroed in on them. They were perfectly shaped. "Touch you. Kiss you." He couldn't help the desire leaking into his voice. "Strip you naked and make you mine." His voice was gritty.

The air rushed out of her. "I'm sorry."

"You have nothing to be sorry about." He released a

shaky breath, breathing through the pain. It was a gnawing ache. He wanted to drag her under him, hear her cries of pleasure.

"And this will just get worse and worse?"

"Maybe." He managed a strained smile. "It's my first experience with it. Other mated couples I know..."

"Sate it." Her voice was quiet.

"I'll be fine." His body started shaking and he gritted his teeth. He *would* control this.

She rose on her knees and pressed against him. She cupped his cheek.

"Kaira—"

She kissed him again.

He wanted to be noble and push her away, but he couldn't. Like in the Mollai cavern, he couldn't find the strength to give up her touch. Her tongue licked his lips, stroked his tongue. Groaning, he fought to keep his hands off her.

She moaned and leaned closer. "Touch me, Thane."

He shuddered. "You don't have to do this for me."

She met his gaze. "It's for me, too."

Her mouth was back on his.

Cren. He yanked her closer. Her head bent back under the force of his kiss.

They kissed and kissed. Even as it fired his blood, it also eased some fractious thing inside him.

Finally, she pulled back, and ran her nose along his.

Thane pulled in the sensation, the connection, the warmth from his helian. They stayed like that, still, faces pressed together, hearts beating hard.

Thankfully, the edgy sensation had eased a little.

"Thank you," he murmured.

Her brown gaze met his. "You never have to thank me for that."

There was a noise, a skitter of small rocks.

They shot to their feet. He saw movement and shoved Kaira back behind him.

She made an annoyed noise and moved back to his side.

They formed swords, both tense, scanning the boulders around them.

He heard the noise again to the left.

A Kantos soldier appeared.

Cren. Thane sensed more life signs.

All around them, more soldiers appeared on the rocks, all still and watchful.

Waiting.

"Hell," Kaira muttered.

Why weren't they attacking?

The first one shifted closer, and Thane noticed that one of its arms was deformed. A battle injury? No. He could see that it looked like it had never formed right. The Kantos also had slashes across its face. Old scars that hadn't healed well.

Thane glanced around the others.

One only had three legs. Another's eyes were wrong, mutated. It only had two glowing, while the other two were empty sockets.

None of the Kantos moved.

"Screw this." Kaira charged forward, her sword in hand.

A Kantos soldier met her sword with its sharp arm.

She yelled and whirled.

Another soldier rushed in and Thane swung his sword.

Even disfigured, these soldiers were dangerous.

Kaira leaped onto a rock. A Kantos charged her and she leaped. She sailed over its head, slashing with her sword. She reached Thane and they pressed their backs together, fighting off the soldiers.

More rushed in.

Stop.

The mental voice made the Kantos freeze.

Thane and Kaira did, too. He gripped his sword, ready for anything.

We mean you no harm.

The first Kantos, the one with only one arm, moved forward.

"You're an elite," Thane said.

I am Nisid.

It had a name? The only Kantos Thane knew that had a name was a defector. And while he might not be a part of the Kantos, he'd still been untrustworthy.

The elite stepped closer and Kaira whipped her sword up. "Don't come any closer."

I've never seen a Terran before. You're smaller than I imagined. The Kantos elite met Thane's gaze. *Like I said, we are no danger to you. In fact, I believe we can help you.*

Kaira made a choked sound.

We are rogues. We are not part of the Kantos horde.

Thane glanced at the others. A small soldier scuttled forward. It was smaller and thinner than the others. Another one had a twisted back.

We were not...created well. The Kantos council dumps us here on Crolla, hoping this planet will kill us off. We are discarded.

Thane pulled in a breath. Kaira's sword lowered.

We hate the Kantos council as much as you. We just want a chance to live. In peace.

"The enemy of my enemy is my friend," Kaira murmured.

A buzzing filled the air and a soldier moved closer to Nisid.

The elite met their gazes. *Kantos patrols are close. We must get to a safer place.*

Thane tensed. *Cren.* Should they trust this Kantos or not?

He glanced at Kaira and saw her face was serious. She gave him a tiny nod.

Thane inclined his head. "We'll come with you. But if you betray us, I *will* kill you."

CHAPTER TEN

They followed the Kantos soldiers.

Unease thrummed through Kaira. She didn't trust them. This could be a trick.

Thane took her hand and squeezed.

"I don't like this," she said.

"Slyness isn't in the Kantos vocabulary. They usually just charge in and overwhelm with their numbers." He scanned the group. "They're all disfigured in some way. I believe Nisid."

The rocky ground grew worse. Ahead, a huge cliff wall loomed over them. Veins of glimmering, blue-green metal crisscrossed through the rock.

Nisid walked right to the wall... And disappeared.

Frowning, Kaira moved closer, and spotted an overlapping gap of rock.

Here goes nothing.

She slipped sideways through the gap.

Inside was a large, hollowed-out cavern. Stalactites and stalagmites in the same blue-green as the veins in the rock outside glowed throughout the space.

Hell, it was incredible.

Thane pressed right in behind her. Nisid settled in the center of the space. Several other Kantos soldiers moved out of the shadows. She saw one with melted skin, and horrible scarring from burns.

Swallowing, Kaira sat on a flat rock. Thane sat beside her.

"How long have you been on Crolla?" Thane asked.

Seven annual cycles. Nisid shifted. *There are some who are older. We find those who are injured or imperfect. The discarded. The Kantos council wants the best soldiers for its armies. They want them whole. Any of us who are not born perfect are tossed here to die.*

Just when Kaira thought the Kantos couldn't get any worse.

"Kaira and I need to get a message to my people," Thane said. "We want to get into the base to send it."

Nisid's pinprick eyes glowed. *Getting into the base is a death sentence.*

"We have to try," Kaira said.

There might be a way. The rogue Kantos paused. *We can help you.*

Thane eyed the elite. "In return for what?"

In return, myself and my people want to leave this planet. We want a safe home where we aren't hunted.

She looked at Thane. *Jesus.* This was crazy.

But it might be their only chance.

You've seen the one path to the base. It's very difficult to get in. We've watched them for years.

"You can get us in?" Thane asked.

Nisid nodded.

Thane rose and held out his hand for a warrior's clasp. "Then we have a deal."

Nisid looked uncertain, then touched his good arm to Thane's.

Kantos and Eon working together.

There is more. Please. Sit.

Thane sat again. Another Kantos appeared, bringing them water, and a plate of dark berries.

Thane tried the berries first and then the water. He nodded at her. "It's safe."

Kaira gingerly nibbled the berries. They weren't overly sweet, but she realized she was hungry.

What do you know of the Kantos Council?

"Very little," Thane said. "Tell me about them. We've never been able to discover much about the Kantos leadership."

A group of nine elite. The strongest and most vicious. They control the entire Kantos horde.

A berry lodged in Kaira's throat. *Oh, God.*

"The council is here?" Thane asked. "On Crolla?"

Nisid nodded. *For the test.*

Thane stilled. "What test?"

Buzzing filled the space, the soldiers around him agitated.

Nisid moved closer. *The council have developed a pathogen. One to disrupt an Eon's bond with their helian. And kill the helian.*

Kaira sucked in a breath. "We saw experiments on one of the battlecruisers."

Nisid nodded. *They have a pathogen ready to test.*

A muscle in Thane's jaw ticked. "We have to stop it."

The pathogen is in the base.

Kaira pushed her hair back. "So, you'll help us get in, get a distress call out—"

I can show you where the communications equipment is.

"You'll come with us?" she asked.

Nisid looked at Thane. *If you guarantee to get my people off Crolla, I will do whatever is required in order to assist you.*

"Then after we get the message out, you'll show us where they keep the pathogen?" Thane asked.

Nisid inclined his head.

"Okay, let's—"

Frantic buzzing. Two soldiers covered in scars rushed into the cavern.

Nisid stiffened. *Kantos juvenile soldiers and bugs are headed this way. They're not ours.*

"We need to go." Kaira rose.

The juveniles here are vicious. Hungry to prove themselves.

Suddenly, a high-pitched buzzing screeched through the air and several flying insects rushed into the cavern.

They looked like bees, but larger. Their furry bodies were black-and-gray striped. They had sharp stingers on their tails.

Go. Nisid rushed forward, his good arm up and slashing at an alien bee.

"Come on." Thane grabbed Kaira's hand.

Several of Nisid's soldiers raced for the exit.

A bee swooped and skewered one of the soldiers with a stinger.

The soldier froze, then its body jerked and shuddered, hitting the ground. The toxin caused seizures.

A bee raced at Kaira and Thane. Thane formed an axe and swung at the bee.

It dodged and Kaira ducked. Thane swung again.

His blade clipped the alien insect's wings, and it hit the ground and tumbled through the dirt.

Nisid's soldiers pounced on it.

Thane and Kaira ducked and dodged to the exit.

Come on. Nisid appeared, charging past them. *My soldiers will take care of the last of them. Follow me.*

They raced outside.

Several of Nisid's soldiers closed in around Thane and Kaira. Like they were protecting them.

Protected by rogue Kantos soldiers. She shook her head and focused on running over the uneven ground. Hell had frozen over.

We have another hideout.

She looked at the Kantos leader. "Where?"

There. He lifted his arm.

Ahead was a dense patch of jungle. It was dominated by the biggest trees Kaira had ever seen.

A wild, harsh howl echoed from the forest, raising the hair on the back of her neck.

Great.

THANE GRITTED HIS TEETH, jogging toward the patch of dangerous jungle.

They had no other choice but to trust their new allies. He hoped this wasn't an elaborate trap.

The sound of fighting dimmed behind them. Nisid's soldiers were fighting the Kantos that had found them.

In here. Nisid waved Thane and Kaira into the jungle. *The juvenile soldiers won't follow here.*

"Why?" Kaira asked dubiously.

There are creatures in here that they don't want to face. Don't worry, my people know their way through here.

The humidity rose instantly, and the scent of trees and rotting leaves filled Thane's senses. He stayed close to Kaira.

They shoved through some thick bushes, thorns pricking at their armor.

They came out in a clearing.

"Oh, wow," Kaira breathed.

Enormous flowers, taller than Thane, filled the clearing. They were bell-shaped, and vibrant in pinks and greens and yellows. A pungent scent filled the air.

Nearby, there were large towers of fungus-like growths.

"It's beautiful," she said.

Do not touch the flowers. Nisid swiveled to face them. *They secrete a deadly poison.*

The Kantos continued on, weaving through the giant flower patch.

They came to a gently flowing stream. A strange animal with giant eyes was drinking.

"It looks a little like a deer," Kaira whispered.

It had long spindly legs, a gray hide, and a long snout. It spotted them, made a clicking sound, then bounded into the undergrowth.

It is a little farther to our base. Come on.

They crossed the stream and reached another clearing. Huge trees, bigger than anything Thane had seen before, loomed above. Their branches spread wide, loaded with dark-green leaves.

They crossed a grassy area.

Kaira stumbled. "What the hell?"

Thane glanced down and saw that the grass had wrapped around her ankle. She tried to pull free, but the grass tightened its hold.

"What is it with the plants on this damn planet? They hate me."

He formed a knife, then slashed the grass to free her.

No! Nisid's frantic mental voice.

Thane swiveled. "What?"

It will trigger a defense response in the grass.

Suddenly, all around them, shoots sprouted. Red flowers unfurled.

"They look like tulips," Kaira said.

Each flower released a puff of pollen into the air.

Don't breathe it in. Nisid was agitated. *Run.*

Thane took Kaira's arm. *Cren.* They sprinted forward, running through the field of flowers.

Kaira started choking. "Can't...breathe."

Her eyes were swollen and red, tears streaming down her face.

"You're having some sort of allergic reaction." Thane gave the command to form helmets. The clear covering slid across their faces, but he still heard her wheezing breaths.

He swung her small, compact body into his arms and picked up speed, following Nisid to the trees.

The rest of the rogue soldiers crossed the flower field.

Thane set Kaira down and their helmets retracted. He pulled out his water bottle.

"Lean forward. I'm going to rinse your face."

She did and he pressed a hand to the back of her neck. He rinsed her face gently.

"That feels better already." Her voice was husky. "The burning's stopping."

The grass here is very aggressive. Nisid hovered. *Are you all right, Terran?*

"Yes. And my name is Kaira."

Nisid was silent for a moment. *Kaira.*

"And I'm Thane. Medical Commander Thane Kann-Eon."

Nisid inclined his head. *Our base is close. You can rest there.*

Thane moved to lift Kaira again but she pressed a hand to his chest. "I can walk, Thane."

He smiled. "I like carrying you."

A strange look crossed her face. "I like you carrying me, too."

He tucked some of her hair behind her ear, then stroked the edge of her swollen eye, wiping away the remnants of her tears.

He stayed close as Nisid led them deeper into the trees.

The jungle and its wildlife help to protect our base.

A second later, the Kantos leader motioned upward, and Thane lifted his head. He sucked in a breath.

Wooden platforms and walkways had been built in the tops of the trees.

"A treehouse village." Kaira grinned. "Every little kid's idea of fun."

A ramp was lowered down, and they walked up into the canopy of the huge, alien trees. More rogue soldiers bustled around.

The place was incredible. Nisid led them to a large, circular platform ringed by a wooden railing. Some sort of gathering place. Other walkways led off it.

Thane noted lots of domed structures dotted around the treetops. Individual cabins. He saw some smaller Kantos wandering around, peeking looks at them. Juveniles.

Nisid's people were breeding.

This is our home. For now. We don't kill except for food or to defend ourselves. We have a right to live.

"I agreed to our deal, Nisid. We'll get you and your people off Crolla. To do that, we need to get to the base and get a message to the Eon. Then we steal the pathogen. I will not let the Kantos council hurt my people or Kaira's."

She smiled at him.

The pathogen is well protected, Thane.

"I don't care. Whatever it takes. The bond between a helian and an Eon warrior is sacred. It enrages me to know that the Kantos council are planning to destroy that."

They are driven by the hunger. Ravenous for more.

They lead their soldiers to slaughter. We are expendable to them. If you are prey, like Terrans, you are food. If you're an enemy, like the Eon, then you are to be destroyed.

"I *will* stop them," Thane said. "I'll give my life to do it if I have to."

CHAPTER ELEVEN

K aira leaned against the railing, the breeze ruffling her hair. The ground was far below, the jungle spreading out as far she could see.

It was beautiful...and deadly.

A tree nearby was loaded with tempting-looking, glowing-red fruits. No doubt poisonous. She could also see the field of neon flowers they'd passed.

Squawks echoed nearby, then some screeches. Branches of neighboring trees rustled.

Turning her head, she heard Thane's deep voice. He was talking with Nisid. She ran her gaze over his intense, focused face.

Despite the dangers of this planet, right now, high up in these trees, she felt safe.

For a moment, she wouldn't worry about how they'd get off the planet, how they'd survive. They were alive, and she was damn glad about that.

With a nod, Thane left Nisid. As he walked down a narrow, wooden bridge, his gaze met hers.

"Okay?" he asked.

She nodded. "Just enjoying this little reprieve." Just like their night with the Mollai, she'd appreciate the respite.

He leaned against the railing beside her, handsome face in profile.

"It's good for the body to recover. Nisid's people are readying some rooms for us. We can clean up, eat, get another good night's sleep."

"Did he discuss a plan?"

"He's going to talk it over with his best people."

Kaira licked her lips. "The pathogen—"

The green strands in Thane's eyes glowed. "I *will* find it. It is a risk to my people. If our bonds with our helians are destroyed..." He shook his head, his voice vibrating with anger. "Helians will die. Eon will die. Earth will be defenseless."

And the Kantos would invade and ravage. Her stomach turned over.

"I won't let it happen," Thane repeated.

"Even if we destroy this pathogen, they can make more."

"I don't want to destroy it. I want to take it with us. We can study it and find a way to develop something to stop it."

She nodded.

"Kaira..." He took her hand. "This mission will be dangerous. The first thing I wanted to say, even knowing how you feel about mating, is it has been an honor to be mated to a woman like you. Courageous, good, honorable."

Her heart thumped in her chest. "Thane—"

"I need you to promise me something."

She nodded.

"If I die on this mission, promise me that you'll get the pathogen to my ship. To the Eon."

Her fingers clenched on his. "Don't talk like that. You *aren't* going to die."

"Promise me." His gaze was direct, intense, boring into hers.

"I promise," she whispered.

He touched her cheek, a brush of fingers. It felt electric on her skin.

"Thank you." He stepped back. "I need to check some more things with Nisid. He said someone would show us our accommodation soon." Thane smiled. "And there will be water for a bath."

Kaira forced a smile. "I'd sell my soul to be really clean." The sponge bath she'd managed with the Mollai hadn't quite cut it.

"I'll see you later."

She watched him stride away, and her smile slipped.

He was ready to die to get the pathogen and stop the Kantos.

And to save her.

She knew in her bones that he'd die to keep her safe.

Kaira's hands clamped on the railing. She'd lost two men who had meant the world to her. It had hurt like nothing else. It had left her in pieces, helpless, grief stricken.

Since then, she'd held herself back from people. She sucked in a deep breath. She'd stopped dancing, stopped doing anything for pure enjoyment. During these intense days, since they'd been taken by the Kantos, she and Thane had only had each other to depend on. She already trusted him.

How would she feel if he died here on Crolla?

Pain stabbed at her.

She sucked in some quick breaths. She didn't want to lose him. He was strong, steady, brave.

And she wanted him.

Desperately.

She knew the mating bond amplified those feelings, but Kaira was honest with herself. Mating or not, she would be attracted to Thane Kann-Eon.

He could die.

She glanced sightlessly over at the jungle below. Hell, both of them could die breaking into the Kantos base.

A buzzing sound filled the air.

She turned. A small Kantos with a bent, hunched back stood nearby. It shot her a shy look, then glanced away. It waved an arm to a nearby walkway.

"Our rooms are ready?" Kaira asked.

The Kantos nodded and took a few steps across the walkway, then paused.

Kaira followed.

They moved from one walkway to the next, and then she spotted two dome-shaped cabins, side by side.

A sturdy, wooden door was set in front of each of them, and it looked like the structures were made of some web-like substance, interwoven with sticks and leaves.

Kaira opened the door and ducked inside.

It wasn't big. The cozy, round space had a pallet on

the wooden floor, topped with a fur blanket, and a carved, wooden tub filled with water. A small table held a plate of fruits and some kind of dried meat.

She looked at the Kantos. "Thank you."

With a nod, the alien left.

There was an adjoining door and she opened it. Thane's room was identical to hers.

Okay, bath first.

She willed away her armor and watched the scales melt away. Next, she stripped her clothes off. The water wasn't warm, but it wasn't cold either. She stepped in. She didn't care that it was lukewarm. As long as she could get clean.

She sank into the water. Hanging from a small hook, she saw filmy, white fabric.

A loose dress with thin straps at the shoulders. She reached out and touched it. It was nearly translucent, like it was spun from the finest silk.

It would do. It'd be nice not to wear her dirty sports bra.

She sank into the water and stifled a groan.

If this was her last night alive, this wasn't too bad.

She glanced at the adjoining door, her mind whirring with thoughts and images, wants and needs.

THANE STOMPED into the room he'd been assigned.

He felt tired, dusty, and worried. The thoughts of the pathogen, and what it could do to the Eon churned inside him.

No.

He removed his armor with a thought. The wooden tub filled with water beckoned. Methodically, he stripped his borrowed gray pants off, then leaned over to splash water onto his face.

He wouldn't let it happen. He'd die to stop the pathogen.

And to get Kaira off this *cren*-cursed planet.

He wanted her safe and alive, to live the life she wanted. To do whatever made her happy. He glanced at the adjoining door, then he grabbed a cloth and got into the tub.

He leaned back against the edge. He never thought he'd have a mate. It shouldn't hurt this much to have her, but know he couldn't touch her. To know that he'd lose her.

He dumped water over his head.

He tried not to think about waking to her stroking his cock. To spilling his release on her belly.

With a groan, he splashed water on his face. He had his duty. That had to be enough.

Small cramps knotted in his gut. He groaned and breathed through it. In the danger of the attack, and meeting Nisid, the symptoms of the mating fever had dulled.

He was an Eon warrior. He'd get through this.

All of a sudden, the adjoining door opened and he tensed. Kaira appeared in the doorway, her wet hair loose, and a diaphanous dress covering her small body.

She saw him in the tub and paused. "Can I come in?"

He nodded wordlessly.

As she moved, the dress flowed around her. It was almost sheer, and he could see the shadow of her dark nipples. He bit back a groan.

She reached the tub, a strange, intense look on her face. "Let me." She took the cloth from his hand.

She moved behind him, reached forward and dipped the cloth in the water, then she started washing his back.

Helpless, Thane leaned forward, his chin dropping to his chest. The brush of her fingers on his skin felt so good.

"You have a bruise." She gently touched his shoulder blade.

"My helian will fix it."

She washed his back, setting desire alive in his body. His cock lengthened. If she looked into the water, she couldn't miss it.

This was torture, but he didn't stop her.

"You really believe we can get the pathogen and get off this planet?" she asked.

"Yes." He put all his conviction in his voice. "I won't accept anything less."

Her hands stilled. "You're a hell of a man, Thane Kann-Eon. I admire your determination."

He turned his head to look back at her. *Cren*, she was beautiful. "If we don't fight for what we believe in, for what we love, life isn't worth living."

She nodded. "I want to be with you, Thane. I want tonight to be ours."

All sound ceased. Every muscle in his body froze.

"What are you saying?" His voice was deep, held an edge.

Her strong, unwavering gaze met his. "I want to make love with you."

Her words were like a punch to his body. His cock throbbed.

"I want to explore every part of you." Her lips parted. "We might only have tonight."

It was all a rush in his ears. He couldn't think past his desire and need. "You have to be sure, Kaira."

Her lips quirked. "There's that noble man. I'm sure, Thane." Her hand smoothed over his shoulders. "I'm tired of being afraid."

Lightning-fast, he reached back and dragged her into the tub.

With a gasp, she tumbled over his shoulder and into his lap, water plastering her gauzy dress to her body.

By the warriors. The muscles in his gut stretched so tight. He stroked a hand up her body and cupped her firm breast through the fabric.

She undulated against him, her round ass rubbing against his cock.

"Kaira." His voice was guttural, filled with need. "Tell me."

It was like she read his mind. "I want you, Thane."

He sat up, water sloshing. He gripped her wet dress and with one jerk, tore it like paper.

He pulled her closer and she straddled him. All that beautiful skin, her taut belly, her perfect breasts, all his.

She panted. "I wanted you inside me so much. When I touched you in that Mollai cavern. I wanted to climb on top of you, sink down on that hard cock—"

With a fierce groan, he sucked one dark nipple into his mouth.

"Oh, God." She struggled out of the ruined dress, her hands clamping on his head. She moaned.

Thane tongued the tight, little nub, then moved to the other one. Water spilled over the edge of the wooden tub as she writhed against him.

"*Yes*, Thane. Take what you want."

He lifted his head. "I want to give you pleasure."

Their lips met. It wasn't a soft or slow kiss. She bit his lip, and he tasted blood. Need rode them both hard.

Take. Claim. Possess.

The words pounded through Thane's brain.

He rose with her in his arms, water streaming off of them. He stepped out of the tub and strode toward the pallet on the floor. He dropped to his knees and lowered her to the bed.

By Eschar's embrace. "You are so beautiful, Kaira."

She arched up and he cupped her breasts, then stroked down her small, toned body. It was clear she kept in shape for her job.

He caressed her ribs, her belly, then toyed with the dark curls between her thighs.

"What do you want, warrior?" Her eyes glistened, her gaze dropping to where his thick cock rose up against his abdomen.

"Tell me what you want?" he demanded.

She let her legs fall apart. "I want you to put your mouth on me until I come."

Cren. Need roared. He loved the blunt way she told him her desires.

He pressed his hands to either side of her hips, and dropped a kiss to her belly.

She sucked in a sharp breath, her body arching.

"As you command," he murmured.

Then he lowered his head and licked her.

CHAPTER TWELVE

O h. *God.*

Sensations rocketed through Kaira. Thane licked, sucked, and nipped. Her breasts felt swollen, blood pumping through her.

He made a deep, appreciative sound, then his tongue licked her clit.

Her body jerked. *Oh.* It felt like her heart was going to pound out of her chest.

As he licked harder, heat flowed down her spine. She ached all over, and she'd never experienced anything this hot and needy.

With a growl, he pulled her closer to his mouth, his tongue stabbing inside her.

"Thane." It was too much, but she desperately wanted more.

"Let me watch you." His voice was so deep. "You have no idea how beautiful you are and how much I want you."

She looked at him and the hunger stamped on his

face. He lowered his head, his tongue stabbing inside her, and it was the sexiest thing she'd ever seen.

Everything built inside her then burst. As she fell, pleasure was a wicked, hot rush inside her. She let out a garbled cry.

Body still shaking, she opened her eyes. He was watching her from eyes dominated by glowing, green filaments. His fingers gently stroked between her legs and she bit her lip.

"Again," he said.

Oh, no. She wasn't going alone this time. She heaved up and rolled them both until he lay flat on his back.

Jesus, that big, muscled body was a work of art. Ripped straight from every woman's fantasy. She leaned down and bit his rock-hard stomach.

He growled.

She felt a flush of satisfaction. She did that. She could drive this disciplined Eon warrior to the edge. It was an addictive feeling.

"I want that pretty spot between your legs on my mouth again," he said. "Seems I'm addicted to the taste of you." His voice was gritty. A hot, possessive look flared in his eyes.

She licked her lips and climbed up his body. He grabbed her and swung around.

Kaira cried out. Then found her legs straddling his head, her hands on his hard abs for balance. And her gaze fell on that long, thick cock.

Thane made a humming sound, then his mouth was on her.

"Oh my God, Thane."

His tongue dragged over her—firm, insistent.

She rocked against his mouth. "*Yes.*"

He slid a finger inside her, and the combination of sweet stretch and the pleasure of his mouth had a climax building.

No. She wanted to see him come this time too.

Kaira lowered her head, licking along his swollen cock.

Thane growled.

She ran the smooth head across her lips, tasted salt. That earned her a low curse, his big body bucking beneath her.

Then he pushed his mouth firmly between her legs, and raw sensation shot through her.

Focusing the best she could, she sucked his cock into her mouth, inch by inch. His hands clamped on her thighs.

"*Kaira.*" A guttural groan. It was half curse, half prayer.

His cock throbbed in her mouth. She relaxed and took him deeper.

Then she found a rhythm, desire driving her into a haze-like dream. All she wanted was to feel, and to bring her warrior pleasure.

His groans turned harsher. Then his mouth was back between her legs, working her hard. She writhed, his big hands holding her in place, right where he wanted her.

"*Starlight.* So good. Too good." His words vibrated against her.

She pulled off his cock. "Don't stop." Then she licked

him again, and sucked him back in. She tightened her lips, bobbing, wanting to drive him wild.

"I'm going to come," he growled.

She hummed against him. His hips bucked up, driving his cock deep into her mouth.

With a curse, he emptied between her lips.

Triumph swamped Kaira. His big body shuddered beneath her from the pleasure she'd given him. She swallowed his release, loving every second.

"Kaira." His voice was reverent, deep. Then he pulled her back against him, his tongue stabbing deep.

She groaned. She was sensitive, every feeling heightened. Two fingers plunged inside her and she moaned his name.

His tongue worked her clit, then he sucked on it.

She jolted. "Yes. That. *There.*" She pushed back against him, mindless, just a mass of need.

She needed Thane.

She needed the release only he could give her.

"Come, Kaira. Let me taste your sweetness again."

His fingers hit a spot and she sucked in a breath, then screamed.

"Thane!" Kaira splintered. Pleasure a deluge that dragged her under.

Sucking in deep breaths, she blinked.

Thane's strong legs came into view. His cock was still hard, despite his release.

Aftershocks shook through her. Shit, their Kantos allies had to have heard her screams.

Screw it. She felt too good to be embarrassed about it.

Or the fact that Thane's face was still buried between her legs, one of his hands stroking her hip tenderly.

"Well," she managed.

Suddenly, her body moved and Thane spun her. He pulled her on top of him, their faces an inch apart.

He kissed her and she tasted herself on his lips. With a groan, she kissed him back.

He grinned at her. He looked younger, and so damn handsome.

"I'm not done yet," he warned.

She licked her lips. "Oh?"

Oh? That was the best she could do? Really, with a naked Thane Kann-Eon under her, and her brain fried from orgasms, she couldn't really blame herself.

"Hold on, sweet, sexy Kaira." His hands stroked up her back. "I've lots of pleasure to give you."

DESPITE HIS RELEASE, Thane's body was still tight and heavy with desire.

For Kaira.

For his mate.

She sat up. Just looking at her perfect breasts and the tight buds of her nipples, made him throb.

He wrapped his hands around her waist. She stroked her hands down his chest.

"You have the perfect body." She smiled. "You're the perfect fantasy."

He didn't want to be her fantasy. He wanted to be her reality. "Nobody's perfect."

She scooted back, brushing over his swollen cock and making him groan.

"Perfection is in the eye of the beholder." She traced his ribs, the muscles of his abdomen, making them tighten. "You probably know the names of all these muscles, and how they connect."

He nodded.

Her clever hands circled his cock and pumped it. He groaned her name.

"Tell me what you want, Thane?"

"You." *All of you.*

She pumped him again. "I'm going to feel this."

His gut tightened. She was small and he wasn't. "I don't want to hurt you."

"You won't. And if it does hurt a little, it'll feel good."

Cren. She was seducing him with her husky voice.

She rose up, her thighs spread wide. He stroked his hands down them and she made a needy sound.

She sank down, so the head of his cock nestled inside her.

Thane felt his muscles strain. He didn't take his gaze off her face. "Take me," he growled.

She sank down farther, her teeth sinking into her bottom lip.

"Oh, my God," she breathed. "So big, thick."

He groaned. "You feel so good." Tight, wet. "I can't..."

He wanted to thrust into her, hard and deep. So there was nothing between them.

She pressed her hands to his chest and she moaned. With another thrust of her hips, he was lodged inside her tight body.

Their gazes met. Her eyes were feverish. His probably looked the same.

He surged up. He had to kiss her.

Face-to-face, her body taking his. He'd never felt this good before. Their kisses were frantic, with no control. Her hands slid into his hair.

"Move, Kaira. However you want. However you like it."

Her eyes flashed. "I like it hard."

He groaned.

She rose, then drove down. She did it again, impaling herself on his cock each time.

By the warriors. Lights exploded behind his eyes.

He clamped his hands on the sweet curves of her ass. He worked her up and down, their bodies slapping together.

His need for her was beyond control, but he still wanted her pleasure.

"Touch yourself," he ordered.

Her desperate gaze met his. Her hands slid down her belly, then she was stroking her clit.

Her body clenched hard on his cock. Then she exploded.

"Yes." Her body bowed. Shaking. "Yes. *Yes.*"

He gritted his teeth. He wasn't done.

He pushed up, and heard her surprised gasp. He pressed her to the bed on her hands and knees, pushing her palms flat against the fur.

"Get a good grip," he warned.

She looked back over her shoulder, her knees open for him.

He shaped her ass, then circled his cock with his other hand. He dragged the tip of his erection through her soaked folds.

"*Thane.*"

With a growl, he drove inside her.

Kaira screamed, her hands twisting on the covers.

He pumped into her. "I...can't be gentle." There was too much need riding him.

"Don't stop. *Never* stop." Cries broke from her.

With one hand on her hip, he tangled the other in her hair. She surged back against him, meeting his heavy thrusts.

"Thane." A whimper. "You're so deep."

"Where I belong, Kaira." He kept thrusting into her welcoming body. "I'd go deeper if it was possible. No you, no me, just us."

Her body trembled and he slid his hand beneath her. He found that swollen nub.

"I can't," she panted. "Not again."

But he felt her body tightening.

"You sure?" He groaned. He wouldn't last much longer. "You're taking me. All of me. I feel you clamping down, hot and tight."

"God," she moaned. "Who knew sexy Medical Commander Thane Kann-Eon would talk dirty."

He covered her, his mouth to her ear and his cock still thrusting deep. "Come for your mate, Kaira. Come on his hungry cock."

Her head flew back and she cried out his name. Her wild climax shook through her.

It triggered Thane's release. It felt like getting hit by

something big and unforgiving, and not caring one bit. His body shuddered and his vision dimmed.

"*Kaira.*" His voice was harsh, broken. He jetted inside her, pleasure a hot, electric rush.

He slumped, catching himself so he didn't drop all his weight on her.

Kaira expelled a breath. "Christ."

He turned and pressed a kiss to her shoulder. "Stay. Sleep in my arms tonight."

A long pause. "Yes."

If this was all Thane got of her, he'd take it.

CHAPTER THIRTEEN

Kaira splashed water on her face, trying to be quiet. She took a few deep breaths, trying to push her unease away.

It was the morning. She'd woken up with Thane's warm body pressed against hers, his heavy arm pinning her close to him.

Air shuddered out of her. She'd desperately wanted to stay there, snuggled against him, warm and safe.

Safe. She splashed more water. They weren't safe. On Crolla, they could die at any moment. Then Thane—so gorgeous and alive—would be gone.

That wasn't the only cause of her unease.

She thought she'd had good sex, and sometimes great sex. She'd been married for two years to a man she'd loved and she'd never felt any lack.

But what she and Thane had shared last night... After the first round of orgasms, they'd dozed. She'd woken with Thane's mouth between her legs again.

They'd had sex in many positions that she'd never known existed.

He'd woken her again and again.

That wasn't entirely correct. She'd woken him a couple of times as well.

She shifted, feeling a tender ache between her legs. She glanced down and spotted smudges of bruises on her breasts.

It had been the best, most intense, totally mind-blowing sex of her life. She blew out a breath. She wasn't sure she could deal with all this.

Well, they had a mission to do today. Get into the Kantos base, or die trying.

So, she'd deal, like she always did.

The adjoining door opened and her pulse did a crazy jump. Time to deal with the awkward, confusing morning after.

I don't want to get close to you...just kidding, let's have sex four thousand times.

A naked Thane appeared, a frown on his face. Her gaze went south and unbelievably, her body lit up.

"Thane—"

He didn't say a word. He strode to her, his cock rock hard. Her mouth went dry.

He picked her up and she wrapped her legs around his lean hips. His mouth took hers and she gripped him, kissing him back hungrily.

He gripped her hips, moving her, and then his cock plunged inside her.

She threw her head back and moaned. She was still tender, but that sweet stretch was now an addiction.

He helped her ride him. He stood, feet planted, hands squeezing her ass as she moved up and down. She impaled herself on his cock, again and again.

"Thane... *Thane*." Her voice was breathy.

Another thrust, and she came. A torrent of pleasure swamped her. He swallowed her scream, and a second later, he groaned through his own climax. She felt warmth jet inside her.

Thane ran a hand up her back, holding her tight.

She knew he'd never let her fall. She cleared her throat. "I guess we have a mission to prepare for."

"We do." He gently set her down. "I can hear Nisid and his soldiers gathering on the main platform."

She lifted her chin, and their gazes met.

"Kaira—"

She shook her head. "Don't say anything, Thane. Our mission is the only thing we should focus on right now."

His face twisted for a microsecond, then smoothed out. "You want to forget last night happened." His head dropped. "I understand. I'll go and get ready—"

She closed the distance between them and pressed her hands to his chest. "I don't want to forget. Frankly, that would be impossible."

His black-and-green eyes flared.

"But I want us to survive," she whispered furiously. "I want us to focus on the mission, so you and I survive. You *have* to survive, Thane."

He cupped her cheek, stroking her cheekbone. "I'm sorry if this stirs up bad memories for you."

"Stay alive." She made herself step back, even though she wanted to move closer. "Now, let's get prepped."

With a nod, he walked into his room and she watched that magnificent male body go.

God.

She discovered that someone had washed and dried her clothes. She fingered the gray pants and sports bra. She was damn glad that she didn't have to put dirty clothes back on. Once dressed, she tied up her hair. Thane reappeared. He was already clad in his black-scale armor. She imagined her own armor, and it flowed over her skin.

"Ready?" he asked.

She nodded.

They left their rooms and moved along the walkway. It was hot today, the sunlight bright on her face.

Ahead, she saw Nisid and his soldiers on the platform. They all had green stripes painted across their chests.

I trust you are well rested.

"Yes, thank you," Thane said. "The accommodation was appreciated."

"And thank you to whoever cleaned our clothes," Kaira added.

Nisid nodded his head. *Are you ready?*

"Yes," Thane replied.

"What's the plan?" she asked.

You saw the carts heading into the base. They are filled with supplies. Food, supplies for the labs, metal. The best way in is to hide in a cart.

Thane nodded thoughtfully.

"That's a great idea," Kaira agreed.

My team will hijack one. You will both hide in the cart and I will act as the driver.

"You're sure this will get us inside?" Thane asked.

It will get us close to the front entrance. We will be able to pass through the gatehouses, but at the final checkpoint into the base, the carts are searched. We'll need to ditch it just before the checkpoint, then climb into the base. My people are all marked with green. That will help you distinguish them from the enemy.

Kaira met Thane's gaze. She nodded. "Let's do this."

THANE AND KAIRA crouched behind some large boulders.

Nisid and several of his Kantos soldiers had gone to ambush a cart.

Kaira was rocking on the balls of her feet, filled with tension. Thane wanted to touch her. Kiss her.

He closed his eyes. Their night together hadn't changed anything. It didn't give him that right. He was well aware that their night was driven by worry, fear, and the knowledge that they might die today.

She was no closer to being his.

Mate. Mate. Mate.

His body and helian said that she was his.

His to protect.

His to love.

"Thane, are you all right?"

He opened his eyes and looked at her. "Fine."

She touched his arm. "We've got this."

The rattle of a cart broke the moment. Thane looked around the boulder and saw Nisid, leading a cart in their direction.

"Showtime." Kaira stood.

They moved over to the cart. The shaggy beast pulling it stopped, then stomped its hooves.

Climb in. Nisid clutched the reins of the beast in his good claw. *Stay still and quiet.*

Thane helped Kaira into the back of the cart. There was gear in crates, some sheaves of some sort of grain, sacks that smelled bad, and stacks of raw metal.

They hunkered down and Thane pulled some sheaves over both of them. Then he rapped on the side of the cart.

It jerked and set off.

It was a long, slow, and rocking journey up the side of the mountain. Thane felt Kaira's touch on his side, and patted her hand.

The cart slowed several times, and each time his gut went tight, certain that they'd be caught.

"We must be passing through the gatehouses," she whispered.

He squeezed her hand. At one point, he heard Kantos buzzing close by.

But the cart kept moving.

Then it stopped.

We get off here. Nisid's voice echoed in Thane's head.

Thane sat up, shoving a sheaf of grain off him. Kaira popped up beside him.

"Come on," he said.

They leaped off the cart.

Nisid arranged the dead Kantos driver on the cart's seat. *They won't know what killed him. This way.*

They followed Nisid up a rocky slope to the side. Thane looked up, and his gut clenched.

The cocoon base was right above them, like a huge thundercloud. It was made of a brown, woven substance.

Look.

Down below, he saw carts pulling up at the lower entrance of the cocoon. There were lots of Kantos soldiers milling around.

We need to climb up there. Nisid pointed his arm.

High above, Thane saw several hexagon-shaped holes in the side of the cocoon. A flying bug flew out of one.

Kaira straightened. "Let's climb."

They started up the side. The cocoon was slightly sticky, which made it easier for them to scale.

Nisid moved ahead with ease, using his four legs to full advantage. Beside Thane, Kaira's face was set and focused.

Finally, he reached one of the holes and peeked inside. "Clear."

He leaned down, grabbed Kaira's hand and pulled her inside.

They were in.

They paused, letting their gazes adjust to the gloom.

Lattice-like walls in a pale gray lined the corridor. A dank rotting scent filled the air. It was dark, dim, with a faint yellow glow from lights set in the walls.

This way. Nisid moved down the corridor. There was a humming noise, and to the left, an archway led into a large room.

"God," Kaira murmured.

Inside looked like a hive. There was a honeycomb structure with flying insects crawling all over it, some fluttering in the air.

Come on. Nisid continued onward. The corridor opened into a wider hall.

Nisid paused. *Soldiers are coming. A patrol.*

"Here." Thane darted through an open doorway.

The room inside was windowless, empty. The three of them slipped inside and pressed against the wall.

The group of soldiers moved past the doorway.

Thane...sensed something in the room.

He moved along the wall, staring at the dull light shining from within. The room was empty, so he couldn't work out what he was sensing.

"Jesus, look." Kaira stared at the wall.

Embedded in the wall were larvae. Thousands, no millions, of them.

Younglings waiting to hatch. Nisid looked at the walls. *This is how we all begin.*

Thane turned away. "We need to get to the comms area."

They slipped out of the room. Echoes of noises drifted down the corridor, followed by a screech.

They looked at the end of the hall. There were two curved, ornate doorways.

"What's in there?" Thane asked.

The council chamber. Nisid shifted uneasily. *It sounds like they are meeting.*

Thane knew that he had to get the message out to the Eon. The mission was critical.

Kaira touched his arm. "We should take a quick look. We could gain valuable intel."

She was right. He nodded.

The three of them crept down the corridor. He saw the walls were thin in places, and he could hear through the thread-like lattice.

They ducked into some shadows. Kaira knelt beside him and they peered through the tiny gaps.

He saw nine elites perched on almost throne-like chairs. They were in a semicircle around a shallow pit.

I can project what they're saying. Nisid moved right behind them.

Thane looked back and met the rogue Kantos' gaze. He nodded.

The chamber doors on the opposite side of the room opened, and a group of docile-looking, juvenile soldiers were brought in and urged into the pit. They looked around blankly.

They were new. Young. Unscarred.

"Are they drugged?" Kaira asked. "They're so...placid."

No. Nisid's mental voice was almost sad. *They are yet to receive the hunger.*

Thane frowned. "The hunger?"

Watch.

An elite stirred. *You are part of the Kantos horde. The backbone of our army. You will fight for the glory, dominance, and greatness of the Kantos.*

Kaira swallowed and Thane pressed a hand to her back.

Prepare to be gifted with the hunger.

CHAPTER FOURTEEN

A shiver went down Kaira's spine. *What the hell was going on?*

The nine menacing elite were bad enough, but this entire base was horrible.

The nine elite stirred.

You will conquer our enemies.

You will consume.

You will be powerful.

You will fight for the Kantos.

The nine elite opened their mouths and emitted a black gas.

"What the fuck?" Kaira fought back a hiss.

The hunger. Nisid stared through the wall.

The black cloud engulfed the juveniles. The quiet Kantos stood taller, shifting restlessly. A buzzing, clicking noise grew—harsh and loud—filling the chamber.

Something rose up in the center of the pit. It was a pile of vegetation, and some small yipping animals.

The Kantos juveniles descended on them, ripping and tearing.

Bile filled Kaira's throat. She pressed closer to Thane, and he wrapped an arm around her.

It was so horrible.

The juveniles finished devouring, and milled around, shoving each other, hungry for more. In the center of the space, she caught a glimpse of the stripped sticks, and the skeletons of the consumed animals.

She fought back her nausea. This was what they wanted to do to Earth. To humans.

They had to be stopped.

Nisid shifted. *We should go.*

"Yes." Thane rose.

The three of them moved away from the council chamber. Her brain whirled, trying to process.

This way. Nisid led them through a doorway.

"I expected more guards in here," Thane said.

They're outside. They don't believe anyone could infiltrate the base.

Nisid led them through twisting, curving corridors. They passed some bugs, but they didn't seem interested in them.

Finally, they moved up the ramp and into a small space. It was filled with dark brown consoles that glowed with colored lights.

The communications hub.

"Thank you, Nisid." Thane knelt. A cable flowed from his armor at his wrist and spiked into the Kantos system.

Kaira watched as his gaze turned inward, and knew that he was navigating the system.

She looked at Nisid. "Tell me what we saw back there."

The hunger is the driving force of the Kantos soldiers, bestowed by the elite council.

She eyed him. "You and your people don't have it."

We were deemed unworthy. In the end, it turned out to be a blessing. It left us more independent, and free from the need to ravage.

"Wait," she said. "Kantos soldiers aren't born like that? With the need to invade and consume?"

Nisid shook his head. *It is the council. The nine elites generate the hunger for the glory of the Kantos.*

"What about the other bugs and creatures they breed?"

They have the hunger bred into them from their creation. The problem is that implanting the hunger from the beginning makes the creatures more...mindless. Less able to think and reason.

Kaira nodded slowly. "So they can't breed it into their soldiers, or they'd lose some level of intelligence."

Correct.

"I'm in." Thane's toneless voice. "I'm sending the message now. It will take three minutes to complete."

Kaira shifted. She wanted this done.

Next up, pathogen.

A buzzing started outside in the corridor. *Shit.* She ducked down and peeked around the doorway. Her stomach knotted.

"Four Kantos soldiers incoming."

"I need more time," Thane said.

"They might pass by." They didn't look hurried, like they were coming to find them. *Go past, you ugly bugs.*

Nisid moved beside her. She morphed a sword.

The soldiers passed the doorway and she held her breath. There was nowhere for Thane to hide. If they looked in...

The last soldier passed, and Kaira's shoulders slumped. *Thank God.*

"One more minute," Thane murmured.

Kaira resisted the urge to tap her toe. She knew once the message was complete, the Kantos would know they were here.

The pathogen lab is in the center of the base.

She nodded to Nisid. "We'll get there."

We will encounter resistance.

"We'll get there, Nisid."

The rogue shifted on his four legs and nodded.

"Nisid, I think—"

A Kantos soldier flew through the door, then stumbled to a halt. Its eyes glowed, and she got the distinct impression it was shocked to see them.

Fuck. She had to stop it alerting the others.

Kaira and Nisid leaped together. He pinned the soldier down.

"Hold it, Nisid." She lifted her sword, preparing to stab it.

The rogue strained against the soldier. The soldier bucked, knocking Nisid off.

The soldier rolled and slammed into Kaira.

She fell and found herself face-to-face with the alien.

It buzzed wildly. Then its sharp arm flashed, and pierced her side.

She grunted and rolled. She got her sword up.

"Kaira!" Thane yelled.

"I'm fine."

Nisid closed in on the soldier, blocking the door.

"Nisid, now," Kaira yelled.

They rushed it together. The rogue Kantos slammed the soldier into the console, and Kaira swung.

Her sword pierced the soldier's neck. She shoved, and green blood gushed. It slumped and she yanked her sword back.

"Thanks, Nisid."

Thane appeared. "Your side?"

She glanced down and saw the blood. "It's not bad. The message?"

Thane smiled. "Sent."

We need to leave. Nisid moved to the door. *We must be gone before more soldiers arrive. They'll hunt us.*

"Let's get to the lab." Thane pressed a bandage from his small med kit to her side.

She smiled at him. There was no way to separate the doctor and warrior.

They moved into the corridor. At the far end, several soldiers appeared.

Thane cursed.

You two, go. Nisid raised his good arm. *I'll cause a diversion.*

Thane and Kaira hesitated.

Go! Nisid charged down the hall. *I'll find you.*

"Come on." Thane pulled her in the opposite direction.

"ARE WE GOING THE RIGHT WAY?"

Thane glanced at Kaira. "Yes. We're heading deeper into the base." He studied the maze of corridors ahead.

They still needed to go down more levels.

"Do you think Nisid is okay?" she asked.

"Yes. He's tough and persistent." They would never have come this far without the rogue Kantos as an ally.

"This way." Thane led them down another corridor. "We need to find a ramp or stairs downward—"

Buzzing.

"Uh-oh," she muttered.

Get the intruders.

An elite's deep voice boomed in their heads.

They swiveled. An elite and a dozen soldiers appeared at the other end of the corridor.

"Run!" Thane snapped.

They sprinted away and reached a *T* junction.

"Go left."

A black bug appeared and Kaira almost tripped over it. They leaped over it and didn't slow down.

She glanced back. "Thane, they're gaining."

The buzzing got louder, like static in their ears. He gritted his teeth.

They arrived at another junction. "Right."

They turned again.

"Shit," Kaira said.

She windmilled her arms. Thane almost ran into her.

The floor ahead was dotted with huge circular holes.

A flying bug appeared out of one, then flew upward. There were more circles in the ceiling, and it disappeared through another hole.

"We could jump across," she said dubiously.

The strips of floor between the holes were tiny. It would be risky to try and jump on them.

Thane looked down. He was excruciatingly conscious that their pursuers were getting closer.

There was a net hanging below.

"I think we should go down. That gets us closer to the pathogen lab, anyway."

She dragged in a breath. "Let's do it."

He wrapped his arms around her, and leaped into the hole, feet first.

"God." She pressed her face against his chest. They hit the net and bounced, then landed on it.

Thane landed on his back and stuck.

"What the hell?" Behind him, Kaira twisted. She was on her side.

It wasn't a net, it was a web.

"I can't move." She wrenched on her arm, but stayed stuck.

Thane tried to roll, but his back was stuck fast.

"Argh," Kaira growled. "I hate the Kantos and all their bugs." A pause. "Nisid and his people excluded, of course."

Thane formed a knife, but couldn't move enough to cut the web.

Kaira was partly on her side, and he saw that she was looking down through the net. "Oh, shit."

"Kaira?" He didn't like the tone of her voice.

"The entire floor is covered in eggs."

"Eggs?"

"Yes. I've seen them before. The Kantos assassins had a bunch of them near the Woomera Range Complex. When they were after Finley." She paused again. "They hatch nasty spiders."

Thane muttered a curse. "We need to get free—"

An earsplitting screech.

It sent ice through his veins. He swiveled his head and heard Kaira gasp.

A huge spider slowly emerged from the shadows at the edge of the web

"I'm guessing that's mama," Kaira said. "I've decided I hate spiders with a fiery, burning passion."

"Stay still," he murmured.

The spider was pure white, with long legs, and giant, black eyes. It had armor plating across its body and abdomen.

"Is that metal armor?" Kaira breathed.

"It appears so."

The web bowed slightly as the spider moved toward them. Its row of black eyes stared at them intently.

"Thane, do you have a plan?" she asked, voice urgent.

He dragged in a breath. "Yes." He morphed a flamethrower.

He could move just enough that he aimed fairly close to the giant spider.

He fired.

The flames shot out.

It wasn't a direct shot, but the spider screeched and darted back a step. The web rocked wildly.

He hadn't hit it dead on, but it had felt the burn.

"Flamethrower, flamethrower." He sensed Kaira trying to move. "Form, damn you."

"Relax. Don't force your thoughts."

"It's hard to relax right now, warrior," she growled.

Despite the circumstances, Thane felt the urge to laugh.

He moved the flamethrower around as much as he could with his limited movement. A sharp, acrid scent filled the air, like burning hair.

He noticed a patch of web start to melt.

"Kaira! The flames are melting the web."

"Got it." He heard her flamethrower activate.

The spider gathered its courage and darted forward. It hit the melted hole and several of its legs fell through it. It thrashed and the web bounced crazily.

"Kaira!"

"Hang on."

Thane felt heat singe close to his side. Then the web below him was gone.

They fell downward.

And landed in a pile of brown eggs.

"Ugh." Kaira sat up.

Above them, the spider was tangled in its own web. Below them, the floor was covered in eggs the size of his head.

Nearby, the top of one of the eggs unfurled.

"Oh, fuck." Kaira scrambled to him, her face frantic. "We need to go. Now!"

He watched a small spider climb out of the egg. Several more eggs started to open.

Kaira yanked on his arm. He leaped up, and together they ran.

CHAPTER FIFTEEN

K aira's chest heaved as she sprinted as fast as she could.

She and Thane powered through an arched doorway.

"That way." Thane pointed.

They skidded around the corner and into a curved corridor. Kaira didn't want to face a horde of small, ravenous spiders.

"Sabin and I fought a group of these spiders on Earth." She shuddered. "We can't let them catch up."

The corridor opened into a large space, filled with people-sized cocoons.

Oh, shit. "What now?"

Thane slowed. "Most are empty. The rest seem to have hibernating creatures in them." Then his head whipped around.

She saw a mass of small spiders fill the end of the corridor. They were on the floor, the walls, clinging to the ceiling. They were coming like a giant wave.

Her lungs locked. "Thane."

"Come on." He tugged her deeper into the maze of cocoons.

Then he stopped and touched one. The top of it opened.

The cocoon was empty, except for a few inches of brown liquid that lay, fetid, along the bottom. It smelled like a clogged drain.

"Get in," he said.

She jerked her head around and stared at him. "What?"

"We're going to hide in here." His jaw was tight.

Kaira grimaced. "Hell." She threw her leg over the edge and climbed in. The liquid clung to her armor.

"So gross."

"Gross is better than dead."

She lay down, trying not to imagine what the goop was made out of.

Thane shifted in beside her. He lay down, and the top closed over them. She breathed shallowly, trying not to panic. Thane lay beside her, the steady beat of his heart under her ear.

If those spiders found them...

"The smell should mask our scent," he murmured, running a hand up her back.

She nodded. "I hope you're right." She wondered if Nisid was okay.

A noise.

She froze.

A second later, a small shadow jumped onto the top of the cocoon.

She watched the spider skitter across the top, then pause.

Another leaped on. Then another. She held her breath. *Nothing to see here.*

It felt like forever, but finally the spiders moved off.

"Keep still," he murmured. "We need to wait long enough to ensure they're gone."

"The Kantos would know we got a message out by now. The soldiers will be searching for us."

"Yes, but they'd expect us to get *out*, not head into the heart of the base." He cocked his head. "I think it should be safe now."

He pushed the top of the cocoon open a few inches, and they cautiously looked around.

There were no hungry, alien spiders waiting for them.

They climbed out, the brown liquid clung to them. She wrinkled her nose. *Ew.*

Thane touched her jaw. "Despite the smell, you're still the most beautiful thing I've seen."

She shook her head at him, but smiled.

The pair of them cautiously moved out of the cocoon room.

"The lab should be up ahead," he said.

She followed immediately behind him. He stopped at another arched doorway, and they looked in.

A Kantos lab. Similar to the one on the battlecruiser, but far larger.

"No scientists." Thane moved inside. "Come on."

They passed several workbenches, some large tanks, and a table topped with gelatinous blobs sitting on trays.

She scanned the room, and suddenly went still. "Thane."

The wall was filled with long, glass tubes, containing similar helian experiments as they'd seen on the Kantos ship.

A muscle ticked in Thane's jaw as he took in the dying helians.

Then she spotted a holder with several vials of a multicolored liquid in it. "Is this it?"

They moved closer. It was milky-white liquid, shot through with blue, green, purple and gold.

"That's it," Thane breathed. "The pathogen."

"There are nine vials."

He took one and held it up. "We'll keep one and destroy the others."

"How?"

He slid the vial into a pouch on his belt. Then he held up his arm and morphed his flamethrower. "Like this."

Kaira stepped back and watched the stream of fire engulf the pathogen vials.

The glass melted away, and then the pathogen burned, turning the flames into a kaleidoscope of colors.

Next, he turned and aimed at the dying helians on the wall.

"Have your peace now," he murmured.

Finally, the flames cut off.

She pressed against his back, sensing his distress and sadness. She wanted to comfort him.

He spun and wrapped an arm around her, squeezed

gently. "We need to move. Now, we can look at finding a way out."

"You sure that vial is safe on your belt?"

"The container appears to be made of a toughened glass. It would require heat or a significant blow to break it."

They jogged out of the lab.

Eon, there is nowhere for you to hide.

Kaira clutched her head. The multiple elite voices felt like a giant hand squeezing her brain.

We will hunt you down. We will destroy you and your Terran. Then we will consume her world and shatter the Eon Empire.

"Such pleasant people," Kaira said.

Thane scowled.

Noises echoed ahead of them, and they stopped. A group of bugs skittered into view. They looked like cockroaches on steroids, with sleek, brown bodies. Except they had teeth. Lots of teeth.

"Back," Thane bit out.

They backed up.

Then she heard noises behind them. They swiveled, and saw a group of Kantos soldiers appear.

"Down here." She ran into a side corridor.

"I sense bugs converging on all sides of us," Thane said.

Her stomach dropped. "What do we do?"

"I don't know, but I *will* get you out of here, Kaira."

GET KAIRA OUT.

Get Kaira out.

He *would* save his mate.

Thane pulled Kaira down another corridor. Flying bugs flew at them from nowhere, wings flapping so fast they were a blur.

They ducked under them. Thane spotted holes in the ceiling. That had to be where the bugs had come from.

"Up!" He gripped Kaira's waist and tossed her upward.

She gripped the edge of the hole and pulled herself up. Thane bent his legs and leaped.

He flew up through the hole and landed in a crouch.

"Come on." She was already climbing up the wall, and disappeared through another hole.

Thane jumped again, caught the lip of the hole, and followed. They continued making progress upward, until they ended up in a large room. A horrible smell slammed into his senses.

Kaira held her nose, her eyes watering.

"Helmet," he said.

They both formed their helmets, his helian providing filtered air for them.

A huge, brown pile of waste sat in the middle of the room. Several small, compact beetles were crawling all over it.

"It's the organic waste generated by the bugs in the base," he said.

"Trying not to vomit here."

"Look." He nodded his head. "There's a ramp on the far side."

They stuck to the wall, moving slowly so they didn't gain the attention of the beetles.

"Thane, if we keep moving up, then what? We'll end up at the top of the base, with no way off. We'll be sitting ducks."

He frowned. "Sitting ducks? Ducks are a bird on your world. Is it bad when they sit?"

She waved a hand. "It's an Earth expression. We'll be targets, with no options."

"The Kantos are hunting us. We have to do what they'd least expect."

"Nisid didn't find us," she said quietly.

No. Thane felt a punch of sorrow. It was likely that their ally hadn't made it.

All the alien had wanted was a chance to live—free of fear.

They reached the ramp and jogged up. On the next level, they retracted their helmets, and thankfully the stench had lessened.

"Let's—"

A familiar, buzzing hum.

"Soldiers," she hissed.

They both scanned for options. He spotted several, shadowed alcoves set low in the wall.

"In there."

They crouched and squeezed in. Kaira was practically in his lap. Thane pulled them back as far as they could go, and prayed to the warriors that the Kantos wouldn't see them.

Several scaly legs stopped in front of their hiding spot.

Kaira tensed.

A second later, the soldiers moved on.

She released a breath. "Thank God."

Thane tipped her chin up and kissed her. When she kissed him back, he felt a bright burst of warmth in his chest. "Let's keep moving."

She scrambled out and he followed. Once again, he was astounded at the strength and courage in this small, Terran woman.

They moved down the hall, alert and tense.

"If I get home, the first thing I want is a giant bowl of ice cream," Kaira murmured.

"*When* you get home." He nodded, indicating a right turn. "What's ice cream?"

Her eyes widened. "The *greatest* thing ever invented." She grinned. "A sweet treat. I'll get some for you. You'll love it."

"I look forward to trying it someday." If they survived. If Kaira even wanted to see him after this.

"Thane, over there."

A set of stairs.

They jogged up them. There was a trapdoor at the top and he pushed it open.

It opened onto a flat area at the top of the base. The bright sunlight made him blink.

"Thank God, fresh air." Kaira climbed out. "I thought we'd never get away from the Kantos stench."

They moved across the top of the base to the edge. There were no railings.

"Oh, boy." Kaira stepped back. "That's a long way down."

Thane stared at the Kantos far below. There was no way off the top of the base.

An idea formed, but his gut churned. It was risky.

"What are you thinking?" she asked.

He glanced at her and she eyed him intently. His reluctant mate was getting used to reading him. He touched the pathogen vial at his waist. He had to get it to the *Rengard*. No matter what.

"Thane?" she prompted.

"We have to jump," he said.

Her eyes shot wide. "What?"

"My helian can create wings between our arms and bodies."

"Like a wing suit." She glanced over the edge.

"It will—"

The trapdoor they'd just used opened. A Kantos soldier climbed out, its gaze on them.

"Fuck," Kaira muttered.

Thane's pulse pounded. Another trapdoor opened and more Kantos appeared. "It won't give us powered flight, but it will help us control our glide."

"Damn." She bit her lip. "I'm not trained. I don't know if I can—"

He grabbed her arms. "You can do anything, Kaira. You've powered through this entire ordeal without flinching. You're the bravest woman I know."

Her face softened.

The soldiers picked up speed, rushing toward them.

"Thane—"

Time was up. He wouldn't let them have her.

He grabbed her and leaped.

Kaira screamed. Thane formed his wings, and felt them snap tight. Kaira's formed, as well.

"Oh, God. Oh, God." She chanted the words.

"Ready?" The wind rushed into their faces. He had to let her go because together they were too heavy for his wings alone.

"No, but do it."

It was so hard to do, but he released her.

She dropped, then glided up. He heard her laugh.

Thane tilted, aiming away from the base.

They needed to find a safe place to land, then avoid any Kantos pursuers.

There was a whapping noise behind them. *Whap. Whap. Whap.*

He glanced back and saw several huge flying bugs, with large flapping wings, chasing them.

Cren. "Kaira, watch out—"

One of the creatures flew right at her and snatched her out of the air. She was clutched in its claws.

"Kaira!"

A second later, a heavy weight crashed into Thane. The flying Kantos screeched.

He struggled, the creature's claws pricking through his armor.

Then the alien wheeled around, taking him back to the Kantos base.

CHAPTER SIXTEEN

K aira was unceremoniously dropped onto the roof of the base. She hit hard and rolled.

She fought back the panic rushing through her. Thane was dropped not far away, hitting the ground with a groan.

Immediately, several soldiers rushed to surround him. They rained blows down on his body.

"No!" She pushed up and ran at them. She formed a sword and attacked the closest soldier.

Something slammed into her, and she fell.

Several soldiers towered over her, sharp arms pointed at her.

Kaira ground her teeth together, and let her sword melt away. She glared at the soldiers before looking for Thane. Her heart clenched. He was on his hands and knees. He spat out a mouth full of blood on the ground.

"Thane." She tried to move toward him, but the Kantos soldiers stopped her.

He lifted his head. One eye was swelling and blood

trickled from the corner of his mouth. Her belly clenched to a tight point. *Assholes*. She wanted to tear into them.

She hated seeing Thane hurt. Her throat closed. Despite everything, and all her best intentions, she'd fallen in love with Thane Kann-Eon.

She'd tried so hard to barricade her heart, but he hadn't bashed through. No, he'd been like water. A relentless flow against the defenses she'd built, wearing them away. And now he owned a piece of her heart.

Now, she might lose him.

The Kantos would kill them. God, she'd been so stupid. Fighting the attraction between them all this time. She'd been stupid not to cherish every moment they had together.

A soldier shoved her forward. When she reached Thane, she had to stop herself from reaching for him. Buzzing filled the air as the soldiers talked with each other.

"You okay?" His voice was a low, hoarse croak.

"Yes," she murmured. "The pathogen?"

"The vial's still intact. Stay alert. We'll watch for a chance to escape."

She bit her lip and nodded. They were surrounded by dozens of Kantos soldiers. She couldn't see how they were going anywhere.

"Why haven't they blocked your helian?" she whispered.

"I don't know, but it gives us a better chance."

Suddenly, she was picked up by the back of her neck. Two soldiers lifted Thane by his arms as others moved in close.

They were led back into the base and marched through the corridors.

Heavy dread settled on her like the awful stench of the place. Finally, the ornate, double doors of the council chamber came into view. Her chest locked.

She and Thane were carried into the chamber and dumped on the floor.

She reached out to touch Thane's arm. They both looked up.

The nine elites watched them with hard, glowing gazes. She got the sense these elites were old. Their gray skin was stretched tight over their bodies.

We warned you that you would not escape.

She winced at the echo of their mental voices.

"Yeah, yeah," she said. "Get on with it."

Buzzing filled the chamber.

You are in no position to be insolent, Terran.

She shot them a sharp grin. "You haven't seen anything yet."

We look forward to decimating your planet.

She kept her face impassive, but inside, her stomach churned.

"The Eon Empire will not let your wanton destruction continue," Thane said. "You will be stopped."

No. The Eon will be powerless to stop the might of the Kantos horde.

"Yada, yada." Kaira rolled her eyes. She wasn't going to kneel here and let them see her fear.

The Eon warriors will be left with nothing without their helians.

Thane snarled. "We will *never* allow you to sever the

bonds with our helians. You underestimate us. And you underestimate our allies."

The group of elite flowed forward. Like a pack of sharks.

Kaira tensed, watching as a few stopped by Thane.

"Leave him alone," she snapped.

One elite snatched the pathogen vial off Thane's belt. It held it up in its clawed hand.

This will be the downfall of the Eon.

Thane glared at the elite.

We haven't yet finished our tests. The elite's eyes flashed. *And you will be the perfect test subject, warrior.*

No! Kaira's heart literally stopped. She watched the color drain from Thane's face.

She surged up.

An elite caught her throat in its claw. It lifted her off her feet and she kicked. She tried desperately to get free.

She choked. She couldn't draw a breath. She felt the tips of the claws cutting into her skin, blood sliding down her neck.

There is nothing you can do, Terran, except witness the might of the Kantos.

"Kaira!" Thane yelled. "Let her go."

Her lungs were burning, the strength leaking out of her body.

Then the elite tossed her and she crashed to the ground. She sucked in some deep breaths.

"Kaira." Thane reached out an arm.

"I'm...okay," she croaked.

Their fingers brushed.

Then they were both yanked apart by the soldiers.

Kaira resisted the urge to fight.

Take them to the lab. Prepare him for the test.

She was shoved forward. Ahead of her, several soldiers pushed Thane roughly out of the council chamber.

A raw sense of helplessness rose in her, choking her worse than the elite had.

She stared at Thane. His face was stoic and he stood tall. She knew that he would never give up. Her strong mate, her passionate lover, the man she loved, would fight until he couldn't anymore.

To watch him ripped apart from his symbiont...

She bit her lip so hard she tasted blood.

She had to find a way to stop this.

But they were alone, beaten, and Kaira was afraid that their luck had run out.

THANE YANKED AGAINST HIS CAPTORS, but they held him fast.

Another one landed a hard blow to his lower back.

Pain rocketed through his body and he stifled a groan. He felt warmth pulse from his helian, as it tried to help.

His helian.

Panic and fear were an ugly mix in his gut. The Kantos were going to try and tear him and his helian apart.

They'd been bonded since he was a child. His mouth went dry. Without his helian, his mating bond with Kaira would also be destroyed.

He shook his head. He had to focus. He *had* to find a way to get free.

He wouldn't let the Kantos hurt Kaira.

Finally, they reached the lab where they'd found the pathogen. One elite swept forward. *Strap the Eon down.*

Soldiers shoved him toward a bench with heavy-duty straps on it.

"Leave him alone." Kaira elbowed the soldier guarding her. She sprang toward Thane.

An elite hit her in the back of the head and she dropped to the floor like a rock.

His gut churned. "Kaira." *Cren.* He was powerless. He couldn't protect his mate.

She pushed up on her hands and knees, and gently shook her head.

Their gazes met.

Cren, he loved her. He loved this woman to the depths of his soul.

Then he was shoved hard and rammed into the bench.

Get on, Eon, or your Terran will pay.

He dragged in a breath and sat on the bench.

"Thane, no," Kaira cried.

"It's all right, Kaira."

She shook her head wildly. "No. None of this is right. I don't...I don't want to lose you."

His heart squeezed, and then he was shoved onto his back by two soldiers. They strapped his arms down, then his legs.

The bindings are reinforced with ingola. The elite's voice rang in his head.

A muscle ticked in Thane's jaw. He was well aware how strong *ingola* metal was. He couldn't break free.

The Eon will regret their arrogant meddling.

"For the love of God, quit grandstanding," Kaira muttered.

The elite glared at her.

Once again, despite the dire circumstances, Thane felt the urge to laugh.

The group of elite moved closer, and one held up its bony arm, the vial in its claw.

The pathogen swirled with so many colors. Thane kept his face blank. He had no idea what would happen. The best case, the pathogen didn't work. But the memory of those dying helians was etched in his head.

He likely wouldn't survive being torn apart from his helian. His symbiont would die.

He had no idea the effect on Kaira. If he survived, he could be left a wrecked shell.

"Thane."

He turned his head. She struggled with her captor and ripped free.

She sprinted for him and gripped his arm. "I wanted to tell you...I'm falling in love with you."

Warmth punched through his chest. "My Starlight..."

"Whatever happens, remember that." She pressed a quick kiss to his lips.

Then she was wrenched away. Cursing, she kicked and struggled against the soldier.

Enough. The elite stepped into view, holding the pathogen vial high. *It's time.*

Kaira loved him.

Thane felt a surge of emotion. His gorgeous smart, strong Terran mate loved him.

It was then he realized that she'd loosened the strap on his wrist while she'd kissed him.

By Alqin's axe, his little Terran was so amazing.

As the elite moved closer, Thane surreptitiously worked on the loose binding. He felt it loosen even more.

He tried not to tense up and give himself away.

The elite stood right beside him now. The pathogen vial looked so delicate in its sharp claws.

Suddenly, a crash sounded behind him. Buzzing filled the air. There was another crash.

Stop them. The elite spun. *Kill them all.*

Thane had no idea what was going on, but he formed a short sword on his free arm and stabbed the elite in the neck.

The alien made a choked noise. Thane shoved with all his strength through the Kantos' hard shell. Green blood ran down the elite's torso. It made another choked, dying sound.

Its claws loosened and the vial started to fall.

Cren.

Thane quickly dissolved his sword and caught the vial, just in time. He shoved it onto his belt.

He half turned, trying to see what was going on.

And spotted Nisid and several of his rogues fighting the Kantos.

Yes. Thane started to work on freeing his other wrist. The sound of the brutal fight echoed through the lab.

Where was Kaira? He couldn't see her in the chaos.

A soldier rushed at him. *Cren.*

Thane abandoned the binding and morphed a sword. He fought one-handed, slashing at the Kantos.

The soldier fell, but another leaped at him. It landed on the bench on top of Thane.

He grunted back a curse. The alien was heavy. He jerked his sword upward and the soldier fell off with a harsh buzzing sound.

He had to get free. He had to find Kaira.

He yanked on the binding. *Come on.*

Another soldier charged, its arm held up like a spear.

Thane's heart pounded and he raised his arm. But he knew he wouldn't have time to create a shield. The soldier would skewer him.

Then the soldier jerked to a halt, like it had hit an invisible wall.

Thane sucked in a breath.

The soldier collapsed.

Behind it stood Kaira, her sword dripping green blood.

CHAPTER SEVENTEEN

K aira raced to Thane and cut his bindings.
Then she was yanked against him, his mouth taking hers in a hard, breathless kiss.

"Are you okay?" she asked.

"Fine, thanks to you." He swung his legs off the bench.

"Nisid found us."

"He has excellent timing."

Her gaze dropped to the vial on his belt. "The pathogen?"

"I've got it. Now, let's get out of here."

Together, they ducked past fighting Kantos. Several soldiers rushed at them, and they both formed their swords.

Kaira fell into the fight. She wanted to fucking live. A burst of energy filled her.

She slashed across a soldier's torso, a diagonal cut opening up. As the soldier spun to evade, she followed, and did the same to its back.

Beside her, Thane lunged low and rammed his sword into the gut of another soldier.

They passed each other, their swords up. On the next swing, her sword slammed against a soldier's sharp arm. The force of the blow vibrated through her body.

Gritting her teeth, she attacked again. Hit. Hit. Slash.

"Kaira." Thane came in low, and she stepped out of his way. He cut across the soldier's legs with a powerful blow. She struck again, green blood spraying across her armor.

The soldier collapsed.

"We need to get out of here," Thane barked. "*Now*."

They ran for the door.

Stop the Eon and Terran.

The elite's voice boomed through her head. Kaira glanced back. Several elites were pushing through the fighting to get to them.

A large, dog-sized bug with large mandibles leaped onto a bench beside them. It snarled and jumped at them.

Thane's sword flashed. With a yelp, the bug crashed to the floor.

Go. Nisid's voice. *Get out.*

Kaira's pulse spiked. *Thank you, Nisid.*

Another bug flew through the air, and Thane shoved Kaira out of the way.

The bug slammed into him.

No way. She watched Thane and the bug roll around on the floor. She morphed her sword into an axe.

"Thane, clear!"

Her warrior rolled free. She swung the axe down, severing the bug's ugly head.

Thane rolled to his feet and grabbed her hand.

They raced out the door, then barreled down the hall.

"Which way?" she yelled.

"Whichever way's clear."

They turned a corner, only to find a massive bug with a bulbous body covered in yellow stripes blocking the way.

It lifted its head and screeched.

"Not this way." Thane backed up.

They swiveled. As they headed back into the first corridor, soldiers were rushing out of the lab.

Kaira frantically scanned around. *"There."*

There was another door farther down. They sprinted into another corridor. A skittering noise, followed by a strange hiss, echoed ahead.

They both slowed.

A bug came around the corner. And kept coming.

It had a long, segmented body in deep brown, with lots of orange legs.

It reared up and hissed. Two long antennas waved wildly, and its serrated mandibles were tipped with jagged barbs.

"Oh, shit." Kaira backed up.

Thane stepped back too. "Back. *Now.*"

They turned and sprinted.

The centipede chased them, rushing down corridor with blinding speed.

"Faster!" Kaira screamed.

Thane grabbed her, lifted her off her feet, and threw her ahead of him.

She sailed through the air and hit the ground. She rolled and came up on one knee.

The centipede rose up above Thane.

"Thane!"

He pumped his arms and legs, then dove.

The alien creature struck like a cobra. It smashed into the floor, narrowly missing Thane.

Kaira darted to him, and grabbed his arm. "Come on."

They raced back down the original hall.

A group of soldiers and an elite blocked the way.

When they saw Thane and Kaira, they stiffened.

When they saw the centipede, they all stumbled back.

"In here." Kaira did a sharp left and shoved through another doorway.

Thane slammed the door closed behind them. Then he formed a flamethrower and welded it shut. "It won't hold for long."

They were in another lab, similar to the previous one, except there was a huge, glass box in the center of it.

She walked over and touched the transparent walls.

"It's a containment cage." Thane touched the glass. "It's made of a diamond-like material. Impossible to break."

Her belly turned over. "It's to hold test subjects."

He gave her a grim nod. "It's strong enough to hold anything, and the Kantos can watch the results of their experiments."

She grimaced.

"Let's find a way out," he said.

A massive boom echoed and the door shuddered.

"Our centipede friend is hungry," she said.

They circled the room. Unlike on the ship, the vents here were too small for them to get through.

Another *boom*.

"We could blow a hole in the wall," Thane suggested.

Boom.

The door bent inward. The alien centipede stuck its head in and hissed.

Break it down. An enraged elite.

"We're out of time." Thane turned to the containment box. "Get inside."

"And trap ourselves?"

"If we're in there, they can't get to us and I have the pathogen. It'll help keep us alive. Maybe by then, the *Rengard,* or another Eon ship, will arrive."

Her stomach was a mass of knots. She didn't like this.

She blew out a breath and climbed through the door into the box.

Thane followed and slammed the door closed behind them. Then he smashed the lock.

There was no way for it to be opened from the outside.

He took her hand. "We've got this."

The doors to the lab burst open.

THANE WATCHED soldiers fill the room.

Out in the hall, he could see that some soldiers had

thrown ropes on the centipede and were pulling it away. It was still hissing.

The elite filed in. There were only seven of them now.

"Looks like you're missing a few of your council," he said.

The elite glared.

They will be avenged. The lead elite stepped up to the glass wall. *Give us the pathogen.*

"No," he said.

"Go fuck yourself," Kaira added.

The elite's eyes glowed. *We can kill you. We can pump your prison with poison.*

"But you want me as a test subject?"

We will flush you out, Eon. The elite turned and nodded.

Soldiers carried a box over to the containment cage. They held it up to a small experiment hole.

Cren.

Bugs flowed into their containment box. They were the size of his finger. They had six black legs, a sturdy body with a green back end, and a small head with beady, black eyes.

As they crawled across the floor, their green abdomens glowed.

"They look like ants," Kaira said.

One leaped and hit Thane's arm. It nipped him and burning pain coursed through his arm.

He flicked the creature off. "They sting."

Several flew at them and he batted them aside.

"*Ow.*" Kaira slapped a hand to her neck. She wrenched a bug off and threw it.

Thane slashed with his sword. He cut through the body of one insect, and green glowing liquid splashed his boot.

"God, it burns." Kaira swung her own sword, and kicked another bug.

Together they swung and kicked. Both of them suffered more stings.

Finally, all the ants were dead. Kaira slumped against Thane, her face coated in perspiration.

"Kaira?"

"I'm okay. Just hurts."

He felt the burn under his skin and knew his helian would be blunting the worst of it.

And this was just the beginning. No doubt the elites had much more torture planned.

An elite stepped close to the glass, staring through at them. *Give us the pathogen.*

Kaira trembled. "Screw you. It'll take more than a few ants to take us down."

So brave. Thane stroked her jaw. "I hate that you're in pain."

She let out a small groan. "Nothing I can't handle." She gave him a faint smile. "With you by my side, I can face anything." She cupped his cheek. "I've been acting tough, protecting myself. But loving someone, having someone you trust at your back, that's worth everything. Every risk."

"I love you, Kaira."

Her smile widened. "Good. I love you too, Thane, and I'm feeling very grateful that you're my mate."

Her words flowed through him. They meant everything to him.

His mate.

He grabbed her and kissed her.

If you're waiting for help from the traitors, it won't come.

The elite's voice made them turn. Thane's gut hardened.

He watched as soldiers dragged in several rogues, then strung them up by ropes.

"No," Kaira breathed.

The rogues were dead.

Thane gritted his teeth. He didn't see Nisid among the dead.

"They just wanted to live." Kaira pressed her hand to the glass. "To be safe and left alone."

He slid an arm around her.

Come out and give us the pathogen.

"No," Thane repeated.

We want you alive, Eon, but not the Terran. The elite cocked his head. *We possess numerous poisons that won't hurt you, but will kill her.*

Thane tensed.

"Don't listen to them." She grabbed his hands. "Whatever happens, we *don't* give them the pathogen."

He met her gaze.

"Thane."

"I...won't let them hurt you."

Her chin jutted. "And I won't let them hurt you. We

fight, my mate. You and I, together. We've survived everything that's been thrown at us. We will *not* roll over."

"*By the warriors*, I love you."

She smiled. "Good." She turned to look at the elite. "Flood us with poison, asshole." She formed a helmet and rapped her knuckles against it.

The elite shifted, looking like it wanted to attack her.

We can wait you out. You have no food or water.

"We got a message out," Thane said. "We both know the Eon are coming."

The elite pulled back, and huddled with the others.

Kaira pressed a hand to her hip. "They're up to something. Some way to mess with us and force us out."

He took her hand and squeezed it. "And we'll face it."

He wondered how it was possible to be stuck in the heart of enemy territory, but feel so good. "My ship will come. We just have to hold on."

She nodded and squeezed back. "When we get out of here, I want a big, soft bed, and a tub of my favorite chocolate chip ice cream."

"Am I invited to this celebration?"

Kaira grinned. "Oh, yes. I'm going to show you some creative ways to eat ice cream."

"I look forward to it."

She stared through the wall. "Look at them. Scheming." She arched a brow. "I hate just standing here, doing nothing."

The doors to the lab opened.

Soldiers brought in Nisid and several rogues.

They were battered, but alive.

"Oh, no," Kaira said.

CHAPTER EIGHTEEN

K aira stared in horror as Kantos soldiers dragged Nisid and his rogues in.

They were lined up, just outside the glass wall. The soldiers held their sharp arms up to the rogues' necks.

Beside her, she sensed a terrible tension from Thane. His hands were balled into tight fists.

Nisid lifted his head. The side of his face was bloody.

We will execute the traitors, one by one, until you exit the containment box and give us the pathogen.

Shit. "Thane?"

"I'm thinking."

"Nisid risked everything to help us. We can't let the council kill him and his people."

"I have no idea when my warship will arrive. If we fight..."

If they exited the containment box, they would be signing their own death warrants.

"If we don't fight, if we don't try to save Nisid and the others, then we compromise our beliefs, who we are."

He touched her jaw. "Have I mentioned how much I admire you?"

She smiled.

"I love you," he whispered.

"I love you, Thane." She was filled with a warmth that washed out her fear.

She couldn't live her life based on fear. She'd already missed out on a lot by doing that. Thane had given so much to her in the time they'd been together. If they died today, at least she'd die living, fighting for what was right, and with Thane by her side.

And loved by an amazing Eon warrior.

"Plan?" she whispered.

"Crouch behind me. I'm going to blow our cage apart."

"You said it was indestructible?"

"Yes, to a strong alien battering against it. Not to a bomb blast."

Her heart knocked against her ribs. "You're going to generate an explosion?"

"Yes."

"How will we survive?"

"Our armor will help protect us, and I need you to generate a shield. I'll leap behind it with you, as soon as I activate the explosion."

She studied his face. "Promise?"

A faint smile, gone in a second. "I promise, my fierce Terran." He met her gaze dead on. "I won't lie. There won't be much time."

"Make it behind the shield, warrior, otherwise I'll be very upset."

He kissed her.

Make your decision, Eon.

She ignored the elite. "And after we blow the cage out?"

"It should generate some confusion. We have to take down the seven elites. Cut off the head, and the rest will lose their leaders."

She set her shoulders back. "Let's do this." She crouched down.

She sensed the Kantos watching her. Thane stepped forward, his feet spread.

God, he was so strong, radiating power.

He lifted his hands.

Kaira watched green energy start to spark between his fingers.

"The Eon will never bow to the Kantos." Thane's voice was loud and strong. "We will stop your wanton destruction."

He was distracting the Kantos from what he was doing.

Kaira lifted her arm, ready to form the shield, but she didn't want to do it too early and give them away.

"And Earth," she yelled. "We stand with the Eon. You look at us as prey, food—" she shot a hot look at the elites "—well, you haven't seen anything yet."

This is pointless. You're trapped, alone. Your allies are beaten, your own people are too far away to help. Give up.

"Never. You're wrong." Kaira shook her head. "Our people stick together. We don't throw our people away like you do. Your soldiers are interchangeable to you, faceless fodder. You throw them at your enemies, uncaring what happens to them."

She saw the soldiers shift uneasily. Out of the corner of her eye, she saw that Thane's ball of energy was growing.

"You have no concept of love." She looked at her warrior and her heart swelled. "And how hard we fight for those we care about."

"Ready?" Thane murmured.

"Always."

Everything happened in a blinding rush.

Thane threw the energy ball.

Kaira tossed up her shield and it shimmered green in front of her.

Elites screamed in her head.

Thane leaped high, over the top of her shield.

The world exploded.

Kaira went blind. The light was so bright, washing out the room. She felt a wave of heat wash over her skin.

Thane. She heard the glass walls blow outward.

Suddenly, he dropped beside her, the back of his armor smoking.

"Thane!"

"I'm okay," he said through gritted teeth.

She reached out to touch him, patting his back. She saw raw, red patches through the holes in his armor.

Then the room came back into view.

Soldiers were crashing into others, and some lay on the ground, shuddering.

Their allies jerked free and fought.

"Let's go." Thane rose, his sword morphing, his face set.

He looked like an avenging angel.

Kaira stepped up beside him, her sword a match to his.

They charged into the fight.

Kaira cut down a soldier. Nearby, Thane was a wild storm as he fought.

She spun. Another two soldiers had Nisid pinned down. She leaped onto the back of one, and sliced across its neck.

As the alien dropped, she leaped free. The other soldier spun to confront her, and Nisid attacked from behind.

Thank you, Kaira.

"Let's get out of here, Nisid."

Thane was fighting hard, cutting through the soldiers, trying to get to the elites. She saw that he'd already taken down two of them.

Stop them. The elites screamed in fear.

Kaira lifted her sword. That was her mate. Unstoppable.

Then suddenly, pain ripped through her leg.

She looked down.

A dying soldier had stabbed his arm through her thigh.

Shit. Blood gushed and she collapsed. It hurt worse than any pain she'd suffered before. The blow had hit something vital.

Kaira. Nisid stood over her, and fought back a soldier.

Thane's head turned. "Kaira!"

NO.

Pain tore through Thane—both Kaira's and his own. She was hurt.

Protect Thane and Kaira. Nisid's order echoed in his head. The rogues moved in around them.

Thane sliced the gut of another soldier and leaped the distance to Kaira. She lay sprawled on the floor, blood pumping from the terrible wound on her thigh.

He dropped down beside her, fighting to find the doctor inside him.

"Fancy meeting you here," she said.

He heard the effort it took her to talk. She was in pain, and losing too much blood.

"Quiet." He probed the wound.

She groaned.

He used his helian to morph a thin black tie, then wrapped it around her upper thigh. It slowed the blood loss, but didn't stop it.

He put his hand over the wound and applied pressure.

If only he had more *havv.*

She met his gaze. Her brown skin was already taking on a pale tint.

"Promise me you'll make it out," she said. "And make these assholes pay."

Thane ground his teeth together and shook his head. *"We'll* get out. Together."

Around them, Nisid and their allies fought to protect them.

"You need to help Nisid," she said. "You need to kill the final elites and get the pathogen out of here."

There were four elites left, milling near the door.

No. He wouldn't leave her.

She gripped the back of his neck and pulled his forehead to hers.

"Whatever happens, my handsome mate, I'll always be with you." Her chest hitched. "Life goes on. It grows and morphs and changes, and we're all a part of it, even... even if we aren't around. I probably should've realized this earlier."

Anger swelled in Thane's chest. He couldn't change this, couldn't help his mate. Here she was being brave again.

He kissed her. "*Live*." He pressed her hands to her wound. "Keep the pressure on."

She nodded. "I will. I love you."

He rose, letting his anger flare and turn into a solid flame inside him. "I love you too. We'll have years to show each other how much." He wanted to believe that.

She gave him a trembling smile. They both knew he was lying.

His sword morphed. His hands were covered in his mate's blood and he wanted vengeance.

Knowing she lay dying, because of the Kantos, made a red haze close over him.

With a roar, Thane charged. He shoved past Nisid and his rogues. With a lunge, he swung his sword.

As he battled toward the remaining elite, the room became a bloodbath of Kantos green. He would spill their blood, as they'd spilled Kaira's.

He saw the elite tense, one of them shifting toward the doorway.

Not happening.

Thane leaped high, his sword overhead. He brought it down in a wild slash, and decapitated an elite.

The other three backed up.

We have more soldiers coming. You're outnumbered. You cannot win.

"I can kill you three, and then your other soldiers and bugs will be leaderless."

More will rise. There will always be more. It is the might of the Kantos.

"You three will still be dead."

He lunged.

With powerful diagonal slashes, he carved into the closest elite.

Protect the council. The mental screams of the elite echoed loudly.

Kantos soldiers and bugs rushed through the door.

Thane kept fighting, pulling on his pain and sorrow to fuel him. "Nisid. Protect Kaira."

Yes, Thane.

Thane spun and sliced. He shoved through a wall of soldiers. An elite cowered, and he struck it down.

A blast of energy hit the soldier beside him.

Thane spun and saw Kaira, her face creased with pain, firing a blaster.

Pride cut through him.

Two elite to go.

But more soldiers crammed into the lab and he was forced back.

He fell into line with the rogues. Hit. Slash. Kick. Stab. All he could do was focus on the fight.

Inside his chest, he felt a coldness growing.

Felt his link to Kaira weakening.

No.

He should never have been given a mate. Maybe it was true that his family was doomed.

He'd failed her.

Boom.

The base rocked. He was almost knocked off his feet.

Boom.

The side wall of the lab...ripped away.

Debris rained down. Bugs screeched and soldiers buzzed.

Thane rushed to Kaira. She was flat on her back now, and he leaned over her, shielded her.

She had a faint smile on her face, her eyes unfocused. It was clear he was losing her.

"I've got you, Kaira."

"I know," she whispered. "I wish we could have had longer."

He clamped down on the storm of emotions clawing at his soul.

Another *boom*.

Something hit his back and glanced off. Light poured inside the lab.

He looked up and his chest locked.

There was a huge gaping hole in the base. The entire side had been torn open.

And an Eon shuttle hovered in the air outside.

The side of the ship opened. It wasn't warriors from

the *Rengard* who appeared. Instead, he saw War Commander Davion Thann-Eon, and his Security Commander Caze Vann-Jad, leap into the base, swords in hand.

More warriors followed, including Lara Traynor.

"Warriors, take down the Kantos!" Davion roared.

CHAPTER NINETEEN

K aira only saw Thane. Her focus narrowed to her mate.

Strangely, the sound around them dimmed, and even her pain had gone away. Well, not away, just sort of a fog that she didn't care about anymore.

"Kaira."

Thane's strong hand rested on her cheek.

"The Eon are here. The *Desteron's* warriors have arrived. Hold on!"

She felt him touch her wound. Pain and sound rushed back in. With a groan, she turned her head. "Nisid...and the others."

"Davion," Thane yelled. "The ones with the green stripes are our allies."

The war commander's eyes widened, but he nodded. "Warriors, the Kantos with the green stripes are allies."

Kaira's gaze snagged on Lara Traynor, and as she watched, the space marine decapitated a Kantos soldier.

Davion attacked the final elite with barely contained fury. Caze was at his back.

All around, Eon warriors attacked the Kantos. A tall, black-haired Terran woman tore into a soldier with a cold look on her face.

Someone knelt beside Thane.

"I'm Medical Commander Aydin Kann-Ath." The handsome warrior smiled. He had black-and-green eyes, similar to Thane. "Looks like you've gotten a little beaten up." The man glanced at Thane. "Good to see you, Thane. Let's get your mate healed."

Kaira blinked, then saw a vial of red *havv* in Aydin's hands. She heard the men murmuring medical terms to each other. Then, a burning sensation ripped through her leg.

"Shh." Thane's arms closed around her. "Let it heal you."

She pressed her face against his chest. Around them, the fight wound down. Several warriors barred the doors to the lab to keep any other bugs out.

The war commander strode over. He glanced warily at where Nisid and his rogues stood together in a group. "I suggest we get out of here before any more ugly Kantos bugs bash down the door."

"With the elite dead, the remaining soldiers and bugs will be in disarray," Thane said.

"Is Commander Chand healed enough to move?" Davion asked.

"I'm feeling better." She tried to sit up.

Thane growled and lifted her into his arms. "Stay

still." He looked at Davion. "War Commander, without Nisid and his rogues, we wouldn't have made it."

Davion looked at Nisid. The Kantos rogue leader inclined his head.

"We made a deal," Thane continued. "In return for his help, we said we'd take them off this planet and find a home for them."

Davion straightened. "Medical Commander—"

"They helped us," Kaira said. "They fought for us."

"There's more." Thane turned so the pathogen vial was visible at his waist. "Nisid told us about this pathogen."

Davion's brows drew together. "What does it do?"

"It disrupts the bond between a helian and an Eon warrior," Thane said.

Startled murmurs came from the warriors around them.

"It severs the connection completely," Thane added.

"We need to analyze it," Davion said. "Find a way to counteract it."

Thane nodded. "I gave Nisid my word we would help his people."

"And we'll do that." Davion waved an arm. "Everyone on the shuttle. I'll task another shuttle to collect Nisid's people."

Thank you, War Commander. Nisid bowed his head again.

Kaira leaned into Thane as he leaped the gap into the hovering Eon shuttle.

"I can't believe it's over," she said.

Thane sat in a chair, Kaira draped in his lap. "You're safe now."

"I can probably sit on my own."

His arms tightened. "No. After almost losing you—" his voice turned choked. "I'm not letting go of you. Not for a long while."

"You going to get all overprotective on me, warrior?"

"Yes. You'd better get used to it."

Warriors milled around the shuttle, sitting or standing, others helping settle Nisid and his people.

"So, we're doing this mating thing?" Kaira said.

Thane's hands flexed on her. "Is that what you want?"

She cupped both his cheeks. "More than anything, Thane. A part of me is still afraid to open up, to lose you."

"I get that, *believe* me." He stroked her injured thigh.

"But I love you more than my fear," she said. "And I think we make a pretty awesome team."

"I love you, Kaira." He lowered his mouth to hers.

"You appear to be feeling better."

The female voice made them jerk apart. Lara and Caze stood beside them, the Terran woman grinning.

"Looks like you kicked some Kantos ass, Commander," Lara said.

Kaira smiled back. "We sure did. But I'll admit, I'm more than happy to hand the task over."

"You did excellent work," Caze said. "Thane, we have a containment box for the pathogen."

Thane handed the vial over and watched as it was locked away.

Kaira, are you well?

She turned her head to see Nisid near her seat.

"Yes. And a big thanks to you. Thank you for all your help, Nisid."

It's been an honor to fight at your side. He nodded to her and Thane.

"I'll go with Nisid and a second shuttle to collect his people," Caze said.

"Nisid, if you need anything," Thane told the rogue Kantos, "you let us know."

They shared a warrior clasp. It was much smoother than the first one they'd shared.

Kaira smiled and leaned into her mate.

"I am very, *very* glad we're alive," she murmured.

"Me too."

"I DON'T WANT to go to the infirmary. I'm healed."

Thane ignored Kaira's protest. The same as he'd done with her protest about carrying her off the shuttle.

He strode down the corridor. The *Desteron* was almost a twin to the *Rengard*. It was a little larger, with a few small differences, but the layout was basically the same.

Aydin's Medical area was in the same location as Thane's.

"You're getting checked out," Thane said.

Kaira huffed out a breath.

Beside him, Thane saw Aydin not even bothering to hide his smile.

"You're lucky your mate is so agreeable to treatment, Thane," Aydin said.

"Agreeable?" She glared at the medical commander.

"Yes, my mate hits. Hard. She's the worst patient I've ever treated."

"She's Terran?" Kaira asked.

"Yes." Aydin had a very pleased, loving smile on his face. "Lieutenant Jamie Park. Space marine."

"The tall, dark-haired woman?" Kaira asked. "I saw her fighting."

"That's her." Aydin touched the door and it slid open. "Here we are."

Thane glanced around. Aydin's Medical was very similar to his own. He felt a pang. He missed his ship and his medical team.

"Set her on the bunk, Thane."

"I'm fine," Kaira repeated. "The *havv* did the job."

Thane set her down.

"Thane's right," Aydin said. "You need to get checked out. *Havv* is amazing, but with extensive injuries, especially when muscle and bone are involved, it doesn't hurt to double check."

The medical commander pulled a large scanner on an extendable arm over. He aimed it over her newly healed thigh.

"This scanner will take a look."

Thane ran a hand over her hair. "I'm needed on the bridge. I need to discuss where to take Nisid and his people with Davion." He glanced up at Aydin. "The pathogen?"

Aydin pointed to a heavy-duty storage compartment.

"Locked up tight. I'm eager to study it, and keen to discuss it with you."

Thane nodded. "Good. I want in on this research." He dropped a quick kiss to Kaira's mouth. "Be good. Rest."

"Go, Mr. Bossy."

He smiled. He knew his way to the bridge, and moments later, he stepped inside the heartbeat of the *Desteron*. There were several tiers of workstations manned by busy warriors. Davion, his pregnant mate Eve, and Caze and Lara stood by a light table.

Thane had only taken one step when a huge dog bounded over and leaped on him, planting its paws in his gut.

"Shaggy, down." Eve moved over, not quite waddling, but it was clear her growing belly was throwing her balance off. "I'm sorry, Thane. He has no manners."

The dog's tongue lolled, then he nudged Eve, rubbing his face on her belly.

The Terran woman smiled and scratched the dog's ears. "Kaira?"

"Fine. Complaining about going to Medical."

"Sounds familiar." Davion raised a brow at his mate.

"Very," Caze agreed.

Eve poked out her tongue. Davion just smiled at his mate, then looked back at Thane. "We have your friends in the cargo bay. Nisid decided the cabins were too confining for them."

"They're okay?"

He nodded. "Aydin will send his medical team down to assist with any injuries." Davion shook his head. "It's my first time worrying about the comfort of Kantos."

"Nisid's help was vital. We would never have discovered the pathogen, nor made it into the base, without him. We also met another species who dwell underground, the Mollai. They helped us as well, but keep to themselves and avoid the Kantos."

"You've had quite an adventure, Thane," Lara said.

"You should both know that the Kantos were trying to abduct you both. I'm guessing they were after your child. They mistook Kaira and me for you."

Davion growled and Eve's face hardened.

"Fuckers," Lara muttered. "They aren't getting their claws on my niece or nephew."

Eve dropped a protective hand to her belly. "I'm afraid we're going to have to disappoint them."

The war commander rested a hand on his mate's shoulder. "I've already spoken with King Gayel and briefed him about Nisid and his rogues. We've agreed to take them to Suderia."

A market world on the edge of Eon space. It had wide-open spaces and was home to a mix of species. "A good choice. Kaira and I saw the elite council on Crolla. Davion, the Kantos soldiers aren't born ravenous. The council gives them the hunger. To turn them into good, bloodthirsty soldiers."

"*Cren.*" The war commander rested his hands on his hips.

"You're kidding?" Eve said.

"I wish I was."

"This is knowledge we can use to our advantage,"

Davion said. "Along with working on finding a way to neutralize the pathogen's effects."

Thane nodded.

"After Suderia, we'll head to Earth. The *Rengard* will meet us there."

Thane's pulse spiked. What happened next for him and Kaira? Her job was on Earth. His was aboard his warship. His gut knotted.

"I want you to work with Aydin," Davion continued. "We need a way to stop that pathogen. We all know that the Kantos will make more."

"We can't let them set that pathogen free," Thane said.

"Agreed."

Thane nodded. "Whatever it takes."

The bridge doors opened, and Kaira slowly walked in.

Thane scowled, detecting the faintest limp from her newly healed leg. "You're supposed to be resting in Medical."

"Aydin gave me a clean bill of health."

The sight of her bleeding from that wound would never leave him. He'd come so close to losing her.

She crossed to him, then ran two steps and leaped into his arms. He caught her.

"Your leg—"

"Is healed."

She wrapped her legs around his hips, and, heedless of the fact that they were in the center of the *Desteron's* bridge, kissed him.

Then she nipped his ear. "Let's go and find an empty cabin, and I'll show you just how healed I am."

Desire ignited inside him, and he barely suppressed a growl.

Eve and Lara were grinning at them.

"The mating fever?" Davion asked.

"Uh, we've already dealt with that." Almost all of it. Thane still felt that constant gnaw of need for Kaira in his gut.

The war commander raised a brow.

"Our mating... It actually happened on Earth. The moment we first met."

"Oh my God," Eve blurted. "That must've been a shock."

"You could say that," Kaira said dryly.

"Luckily, our nice trip with the Kantos convinced Kaira that mating might not be so bad," Thane said.

She smiled at him.

"Kaira, I'm afraid I need Thane a little longer," Davion said. "For a continued discussion on the pathogen."

She unhooked her legs and he set her on her feet. "I understand."

Eve moved forward. "We'll find you a cabin. I'll bet you're dying for a shower."

Kaira groaned. "Like you wouldn't believe."

Eve smiled. "And I'm sure your mate will find you when he can."

"Does this cabin have a soft bed?" Kaira asked.

"Absolutely."

"Earth food?"

"The ship's synthesizers can make just about anything," Eve said.

"Ice cream?"

"Sure thing."

Kaira shot Thane a hot look. "Don't be too long."

He was hard as a rock. "I won't."

CHAPTER TWENTY

Kaira spent far too long in the shower, but the flow of hot water had been way too seductive to ignore.

Dressed in a black Eon uniform, she wandered the cabin she'd been assigned. She'd tested out the synthesizer. It did make ice cream. And it was pretty good-tasting, actually.

Now, all she needed was her mate.

Mate. She smiled. Thane was everything. The way he'd stood by her during their ordeal on Crolla, the way he'd helped her, protected her, loved her...

Kaira was all-in.

The fear of losing Thane—like she'd lost Ryan and her father—would never go away, but she was done letting it overshadow her life.

"I love you, Ryan," she whispered. "I always will, but I have a mate who makes me smile again." She knew her late husband would want that for her.

She had a whole load of living to do, and she planned to do it with her handsome mate.

If he ever showed up.

She blew out a breath. He was a warrior. No doubt there were issues he had to sort out with Davion, and it was taking longer than planned.

Maybe she'd check on Nisid. She headed out of the cabin. She liked the warship—it was sleek, with black metal everywhere, but not cold. It wasn't just a warship, but a home for its warriors.

She moved down the corridor, and suddenly realized she had no idea how to get to the cargo bay housing the Kantos rogues.

"Hey, I was coming to see you."

She looked up and saw Lara Traynor. The tall woman was wearing a black Eon uniform, like Kaira.

"I wanted to visit our Kantos allies," Kaira said.

"I'll show you the way."

They fell into step together.

"I never thought I'd live to see the day when we'd transport Kantos to safety," Lara said.

"Surprised me, too. Working with them." Kaira followed Lara into an elevator. "I guess I got so used to thinking of Kantos as the evil enemy, but nothing in life is black-and-white. I know Thane and I would've died without Nisid and his people. He's earned my trust. I just hope everyone else treats them right."

The elevator moved, and a moment later the doors opened.

"The Eon are fair, Kaira," Lara said. "They'll honor the agreement and get Nisid and his people away from the other Kantos. Suderia is a peaceful world, and will make a safe home for them." She led Kaira down the hall, and then stopped in front of some large doors. "Here we are."

The doors opened and Kaira saw Kantos milling around the space. Some were relaxed, others pacing. Several juveniles were running around, chasing each other.

Everyone paused.

Kaira lifted a hand. "Hi."

Kaira. Nisid broke away from the crowd.

"How are you, Nisid?" She touched his arm.

We are all fine. Medical Commander Kann-Ath visited, and tended to our injuries.

"I'm told we're en route to a world that will provide you with a new home."

He bowed his head. *I'm very grateful.*

"Don't be. You earned it. Without you and your fighters, Thane and I would never have made it. And now, we also have a sample of the pathogen. To me, you're a hero."

The Kantos leader shifted on his four legs, and she got the impression that if he could, he'd be blushing.

Are you all healed, Kaira?

"Yes." She had the shiny, pink skin on her thigh to prove it. "I've been triple-checked, and my leg healed up well. I wanted to thank you again. And wish you and your people well."

Thank you, Kaira. It's been an honor to help you.

She held out her hand, and gingerly he grasped her fingers in his claws. They shook.

When she headed out of the cargo bay with Lara, the

space marine shook her head. "I still have a hard time wrapping my head around good Kantos."

"It's the hunger," Kaira said.

Lara's face hardened. "Thane told us. Nisid and his people weren't given it. The council turn the soldiers and bugs into insane killers. Assholes."

"Thane killed the council elites, but I'm guessing a new council is already forming." The Kantos would keep coming. "They have to be stopped."

"Yep."

"Anyway, I've had more than enough Kantos interaction over the last few days. I'm keen to find my mate."

Lara's lips quirked. "I'll bet. Take the elevator down a level. The last I heard, he was with Aydin in Medical. No doubt, the pair of them are plotting how to stop that pathogen."

"Thanks, Lara."

"Enjoy your mate, Kaira." Lara's face changed, lighting up. "Mating...is incredible." The space marine grinned. "And I don't just mean the hot sex. Having a true partner, someone who understands you, respects you. Love is worth everything."

Chest tight, Kaira nodded. "I forgot that for a while, but I won't again." She stepped into the elevator.

She waved goodbye to Lara as the doors closed. She'd just stepped out into the hall when she spotted Thane. He looked deep in thought.

Then his head whipped up. His face sharpened, the green filaments in his eyes aglow.

Kaira's belly clenched, desire ignited like a solar flare.

He strode right to her and lifted her off her feet.

"Hello, mate," she said.

He didn't say anything, just kissed her.

Heat exploded. She clamped her legs around him. His big hands cupped her ass, and she slid her hands into his gray-streaked hair and tugged.

"God, you taste addictive," she whispered against his lips.

He growled and took her mouth again. She felt the hard press of his erection against her belly.

She rubbed against him. "Thane. Cabin."

"Too far."

He strode down a side corridor and into a shadowed alcove. He pinned her to the wall.

"Need you." His magnificent, black-and-green eyes met hers. "*Now.*"

"So, take me," she said.

His hand moved between their bodies yanking at their clothes. He pushed her pants down, and she dropped her legs to let them slide off.

Then he opened his pants and freed his cock.

With his gaze on hers, she wrapped her legs around him, and felt the hot brush of his cock.

Then with one hard plunge, he surged inside her.

"Thane!"

"My mate. My Starlight. *My Kaira.*"

Then there was nothing but the two of them, the heavy plunge of his body claiming hers.

Kaira moaned against his ear. "Don't stop."

"Never."

THANE'S MUSCLES TENSED. The cold substance hit his abdomen, and he gritted his teeth.

He was naked, lying flat on his back on the bed. An equally naked, very-pleased-looking, Kaira leaned over him, dripping cold, creamy ice cream on his abs.

With a purring sound, she lowered her head and lapped.

Cren. He reached his arms up, gripping the bedhead. His hips bucked up.

"No moving, warrior." She carried a spoonful of ice cream to his lips.

Thane ate the sweet food, savoring the small, crunchy lumps of what she told him were chocolate.

She dribbled more down his stomach, then lower, her mouth hitting his skin and following the trail.

He tangled his hand in her hair. He groaned her name.

Then her mouth licked his hard cock, and she sucked him deep.

As she worked him, desire for his mate roared through him. He knew it would grow and change the longer they were together.

He couldn't wait. Every minute with her was something to treasure.

But right now, he wanted to see pleasure on Kaira's face. Hear her cry out his name.

He sat up and pulled her off him.

"Thane," she complained.

He pushed her onto her back and grabbed the bowl of ice cream.

Her gaze locked on him, her breath hitching.

"I think I'm developing a taste for ice cream," he said.

She bit her lip. "Do you like it?"

"I'm not sure yet. I need a few more tastes."

He dribbled the cold treat on one of her breasts.

She gasped, her cheeks flushing.

Thane licked up the sweet stickiness, taking his time sucking on her nipple. Her breathing turned choppy. He lavished her other breast with the same attention.

"Oh, Thane." She writhed against the sheets.

"Hmm, I'm not one-hundred-percent certain about this ice cream, yet." He let the dessert drip on her flat belly.

She jerked.

It pooled in her navel, and with a smile, he licked the icy trail. He loved the sounds she made. He cupped one hand between her legs, sliding a finger inside her warmth.

"*Yes*. Thane, I'll never get enough of you. Come inside me."

With a final lick, he rose over her. He grabbed her leg, pulling her thigh tight against his side and opening her up to him.

Then he sank inside her.

Their groans mingled. He kept his gaze on her fathomless, dark eyes as he moved inside her.

Her eyes pulled him in, just like everything about his mate did. He picked up speed, thrusting harder, deeper.

"Thane!" As she came, she raked her nails down his back.

With a growl, he plunged deeper and held himself inside her as his own release hit him like a wave.

Finally, he rolled, holding her close. He stroked a hand up and down her back.

Then he noticed something. "The ship's stopped."

Kaira jerked into a sitting position. "We've reached Suderia. Nisid and the others will be leaving."

She scrambled up and raced for the washroom.

Thane leaned back and enjoyed the view of his naked mate. "You'll miss Nisid?"

She popped her head back out. "We owe him our lives."

His Terran, such a big heart. She'd kept it guarded after having it hurt, but it was wide open, now.

Thane would spend a lifetime guarding it for her.

He climbed out of the bed and joined her in the shower. It wasn't long before they were clean and dressed in Eon uniforms, heading for the cargo bay.

The rogue Kantos were ready, the few belongings they'd brought, packed and assembled.

Thane and Kaira moved over to Nisid.

We're ready to head to the planet shortly. War Commander Thann-Eon has arranged shuttles for us.

"We wish you the best of luck, Nisid," Kaira said.

Thank you. He scanned his people. *Now, we have a chance to make a life on our own. Without fear.*

"Suderia is a good world," Thane said. "Many different species and opportunities."

Nisid nodded. *We will do things on our own terms.*

Kaira moved away, and Thane saw her nodding and smiling at a smaller, shy Kantos.

Take care of your brave mate, Thane.

"You don't have to worry about that. Goodbye, Nisid." Thane clasped the Kantos' bony shoulder.

Goodbye, Thane Kann-Eon. My friend. The alien's gold eyes glowed.

Thane stood with an arm around Kaira's shoulders on the observation deck at the front of the ship. Through the huge, glass windows, they watched the shuttles leave the *Desteron*, taking the Kantos to the planet below.

"Next up, Earth," Thane said, lightly.

Kaira turned to look at him. "You worried I'm going to ditch you?"

He swallowed, and reached to tuck a strand of her hair behind her ear. "I know you love me..."

"I do. You think there might be any jobs on the *Rengard* for me?"

His pulse leaped. "We can talk to Malax. He'd be crazy not to find a use for your skills." Thane gripped her arms. "You're sure?"

"I want to be with you, Thane. I enjoy my job with the Air Force, but I won't lie—" a smile lit her face "—I like the idea of exploring the galaxy with you."

He kissed her. "We'll talk to Malax. I promise you the most amazing adventures, Kaira."

"As long as they don't involve getting abducted by the enemy and surviving on a dangerous, alien planet, I'm in."

CHAPTER TWENTY-ONE

K aira stepped out of the shuttle and onto the orange-red dirt outside the main Woomera Range Complex buildings. She felt a little rush of relief. No matter where she went, Earth would always be her home.

Then Thane touched her lower back and smiled at her.

Correction. Earth would always be her old home, but Thane was her new one.

"Kaira!"

She saw Finley, and her assistants, Ian and Gemma, waving at her. Sabin stood behind Finley, his hands resting on her shoulders. War Commander Malax Dann-Jad and his mate Wren were with them.

When Kaira strode over, Finley hugged her hard.

"We're *so* glad you're okay," the scientist said.

"Thanks. I do *not* recommend alien abduction."

The scientist snorted. "We hear you've been quite the badass. Fighting the Kantos, destroying a base, and uncovering a Kantos pathogen."

Kaira shrugged. "Believe me, I'm not planning on being abducted by the Kantos again."

Finley grabbed Kaira's hand. "I *totally* didn't enjoy my abduction either. We're really glad you're back."

"I'm not staying. I need to call my commanding officer. I'll be resigning from the Air Force."

Finley's eyebrows rose.

Kaira looked at Thane. "I'm hoping to join my mate on the *Rengard*."

"You're mated?" Sabin broke out in a grin, and grabbed Thane's hand. "I'm so happy for you."

Thane smiled. "We both got very lucky, my friend."

"We sure did."

"It happened during your abduction?" Gemma sighed. "How romantic."

"Not exactly," Kaira said. "It's a long story."

Malax stepped forward, and the war commander gripped Thane's arm. Then he met Kaira's gaze. His black eyes were threaded with gold. "It would be an honor to have you aboard the *Rengard*, Kaira. I hope you might be interested in a position with the *Rengard* security team. We happen to be without our security commander." He shot a pointed look at Sabin. "The team needs good people."

Her chest swelled. "That sounds great. I'd be honored to join."

Thane hugged her to his side.

Suddenly, an Eon shuttle swept in overhead.

"Who's that?" Finley asked. "Is it from the *Rengard*?"

All the warriors straightened.

"Thane?" Kaira asked.

The shuttle landed, kicking up dust.

"That's the royal shuttle," Malax said in a hushed voice.

Royal? The side door of the shuttle opened.

Two warriors stepped off—one male, one female. They wore typical, black Eon uniforms, but they also wore a blue sash across their chests.

They were both alert; clearly lethal. They scanned the area.

Then, another warrior stepped off behind them.

Oh. Wow.

He was tall, with a warrior's powerful body. He wore a sleeveless shirt in a deep blue, and a gold cord circled one of his muscled biceps. His handsome, rugged face was framed by the typical long, brown hair of an Eon warrior.

King Gayel Solann-Eon strode toward them. All the warriors bowed their heads.

"Your Highness," Davion said.

"It's a pleasure to see you all," the king said. "And meet some of you in person for the first time." His voice was deep and melodious, with an authoritative edge. His gaze—black with filaments of rich purple—swept over them and settled on Eve. "Ambassador Thann-Eon, I hope you and your baby are well."

"We're well, and getting huge."

A smile edged the king's lips. Then he turned to Thane and Kaira.

"Medical Commander, Commander Chand, I'm very happy you survived your abduction."

"Thank you, Your Highness," Thane said.

"Congratulations on your mating."

Kaira fought the strange urge to curtsy. "Ah, thank you. It's nice to meet you."

"You too. I was so glad to hear that you and Thane survived Crolla. And brought back a sample of the pathogen." The king's handsome face turned serious. "It's imperative we find a way to neutralize it."

"We will," Thane said. "We've already started work."

The king met Kaira's gaze. "And you befriended some Kantos allies."

"It wasn't planned," she said.

"They shared valuable information with us. It will help us in the fight to protect Earth and the Eon Empire against the Kantos." The king turned back to Eve. "Now, Ambassador—"

"Please stop calling me that."

The king smiled, and it felt like the air surrounding them all heated by a few degrees.

Kaira blinked. The man was potent to the female senses.

"Eve, I want to discuss the visit of the delegation from Earth to Eon."

Eve did a poor job of hiding her grimace. "Plans are progressing."

"Excellent. I want to make a change."

Eve groaned, then touched her belly. "Um, sorry, the baby kicked."

Behind her, her mate shook his head.

"I've decided, in order to strengthen our alliance, that I will marry a Terran."

Kaira's eyes opened wide. She saw Eve's mouth drop open.

The warriors all went as still as statues.

"I want you to ensure suitable candidates are included in the delegation."

"You want me to find you a *wife*?" Eve's voice rose.

"Yes. I have full confidence in your abilities, Eve."

Kaira met Thane's gaze. Her mate raised a brow.

She looked forward to seeing how this panned out.

Gayel

KING GAYEL SOLANN-EON sat at the head of the long dining table. The senior warriors from the *Rengard* and *Desteron*, and their mates, talked and laughed and ate.

The kitchen of the Woomera Range Complex had worked hard to prepare a feast they believed was worthy for a king. The sunset outside the window of the testing facility was impressive. Red, pink and gold streaked across the vast sky.

He was heading to Space Corps Headquarters in Houston tomorrow, before traveling back to Eon to prepare for the Earth delegation to arrive. He was glad he'd managed this short visit to Earth.

And it was good to see his warriors and their mates.

A sensation moved through his gut. He recognized it as envy. It was a familiar emotion. As a young prince growing up, he'd had a lot of lavish extravagances, always known that one day he would be king. But he'd always envied his people the simple things of life. Things far out of his reach.

Yes, he envied his warriors and their mates. That deep connection between the couples.

His father had been set in his ways, but Gayel had never doubted that the man had loved his mate, Gayel's mother. But mating was rare for the Eon, although their best scientists were working to discover why so many mates seemed to be coming from among the Terrans.

Maybe he'd get lucky and his mate would be one of the candidates for his wife.

He squashed that thought. It didn't matter. He would marry a Terran. The new genetic material to the Eon line would be beneficial, and the marriage would cement an alliance with Earth. He'd been impressed with the Terran resilience, fortitude, and ingenuity.

Gayel had been raised knowing he had a duty.

To his people.

To his Empire.

His own happiness wasn't a factor.

He would do what was best for the Eon Empire, even if he had to sacrifice his own wants and needs.

He hoped he could find a wife with intelligence and compassion, a partner to stand at his side.

Gayel had spent a lot of time undoing the restrictive rules of his father's reign. He wanted to do more for his Empire, to watch it flourish.

He watched Davion lean close to his mate, the two of them smiling. Then he looked at the newest mated couple. Thane and Kaira shared a private look, their attraction tangible.

Gayel lifted his drink. He was unlikely to have a mate, but he would do his duty and treat his wife with respect.

And he would do what had to be done to protect his empire and end the Kantos threat.

AFTER THE DINNER, Thane shared an Earth beer with Sabin.

"You're happy to be stationed here?" he asked his friend.

"I'm happy to be with my mate," Sabin said.

"I understand that." He looked to Kaira. She was laughing with Finley, Gemma, and Lara.

"Look at us, Thane." Sabin grinned. "Just weeks ago, neither of us expected to be mated. You thought it couldn't happen for you, and I didn't want it. Cren, I was afraid of it."

"And now neither of us would give up our women."

"I'd fight anyone who tried to take Finley from me."

"We're lucky."

"Beyond lucky. Blessed by the warriors."

They tapped their glasses together.

"Sounds like your first task as the new Eon ambassador to Earth will be shortlisting candidates for the king's wife."

Sabin grimaced. "I'll leave that to Eve."

Thane shook his head and sipped his drink. "Sabin,

the Kantos won't stop. The StarStorm won't hold them off forever. If we're lucky, we'll find an antidote and stop the pathogen, but the Kantos will invent more weapons, more abominations."

"King Gayel is committed to stopping them, one way or another. With Earth and these resilient Terrans by our side, we can win."

Thane nodded. They'd never stop fighting.

"You two look so serious." Kaira appeared, moving to Thane's side and wrapping an arm around his waist.

"We were talking about the Kantos," he told her.

She groaned. "No Kantos tonight. Tomorrow, we'll have to worry about them, but tonight is ours."

"But we—"

She pressed a finger to his lips. "No excuses, warrior.

Finley claimed Sabin, dragging him away.

"Now, I get you to myself," Kaira murmured.

"I'm yours," he said. "Every minute of every day. No moment will go by where I don't love you, and where I'm not grateful you're my mate."

Her face softened. "Don't make me cry."

"As long as they're happy tears."

"If I'm with you, they will be. Thanks for making me fall in love with you, Thane."

He pulled her close, loving the way her small, toned body fit against him. Right where it was supposed to be.

"Thanks for loving me, Kaira, and gifting me your heart. I'll protect it for the rest of our lives."

They kissed, and it was filled with hope, love, and promise.

She smiled. "Now, how about some dessert?"

He smiled back. "I have developed a taste for ice cream."

I hope you enjoyed Kaira and Thane's story!

Eon Warriors continues with the final action-packed adventure, King Gayel's story, ***King of Eon***. **Read on for a preview of the first chapter.**

Don't miss out! For updates about new releases, action romance info, free books, and other fun stuff, sign up for my VIP mailing list and get your *free box set* containing three action-packed romances.

Visit here to get started: www.annahackett.com

PREVIEW: KING OF EON

He stalked silently under the giant Arcadix. Dappled light filtered through the trees' canopy, and the scent of cassia blossoms filled his senses.

Gayel Solann-Eon paused, cocked his head and listened.

I know you're here.

He felt a pulse from his helian, and his enhanced senses spread.

Yes. With the help from his symbiont, he could hear the heartbeat of the neegall. It was a vicious creature, a hunter that liked to stalk its prey.

But Gayel was an Eon warrior. Clad in his helian armor, his body covered in black scales, the helian on his wrist pulsed again. He'd been bonded to the alien symbiont since he was young, and it gave him—gave all Eon warriors—incredible abilities. For a moment, he savored the sensation of the link.

As King of the Eon Empire, he didn't get to indulge his warrior instincts as much as he liked.

That was why he'd snuck out on this solo hunt.

He climbed over a huge, fallen log. Massive tentra vines fell in a tangle from above. He scanned the branches overhead. Neegalls like to ambush from overhead.

He picked up a foul stench—old blood, dirty fur.

It was close.

With a simple thought, his sword formed on his arm, glowing with hints of purple.

Another step—

The creature moved blindingly fast, launching off from a branch above.

Gayel swung his sword up, but he already knew he was too slow.

The neegall slammed into him, driving him to the ground. Hot, fetid breath washed over his face.

Gayel's sword shrank to a jagged knife.

He and the creature rolled. He tried to stab it, but it blocked the move with a powerful arm.

With a grinding sound, claws raked his armor. Grunting, Gayel heaved and they rolled again, across the layer of rotting leaves and moss.

The neegall sprang off him and Gayel rose to his feet.

The creature was vaguely humanoid, but had powerful legs and a curved back. Both its hands and feet were tipped with long claws designed to rend. It was covered in a layer of dense, brown fur, with a face that elongated to a shaggy muzzle filled with wicked fangs.

It snarled.

They circled each other. Gayel took a deep breath, and kept his gaze on his opponent. His heart thumped steadily and his blood sang. He was a warrior, doing what he did best.

The neegall launched at him.

Gayel leaped.

They clashed. Gayel swung his blade, catching the predator in the gut.

It yowled. With a powerful front kick, Gayel sent it flying and it hit the dirt.

Advancing, he never shifted his gaze off his foe. The neegall rose, and gave a vicious howl.

With a burst of movement, Gayel attacked. *Swing, slice, stab.*

His blade slid between the creature's ribs and hit one of its two hearts.

The creature made a coughing sound, and collapsed.

Gayel stepped back, sucking in air and smiling.

Cren, he didn't get to do this enough. Since he'd become king after the death of his father, he'd been dedicated to his people, to the Eon Empire.

That meant endless meetings, dinners, diplomatic

missions, trade negotiations. It also meant dealing with security concerns as their enemy, the Kantos, loomed.

With a sigh, he cleaned off his knife.

The sound of a twig snapping made him spin.

A woman in full armor, sword in hand, stepped out of the trees.

She scowled at him. "You don't sneak off from your personal guard, Your Highness."

When she said "Your Highness" with that tone of voice, he was fairly sure she meant, *you idiot*. There was distinct annoyance in her voice and in eyes that echoed his own—fathomless black threaded with purple filaments.

She had the same deep-brown hair, as well. Most Eon looked alike, and there wasn't much variation in their species, but Adlyn looked even more like him, since she was his sister.

"We're in the Sanguinis Wood, right outside our shining capital." Gayel dissolved his blade with a single thought. "What risk is there here?"

She shot the neegall a pointed look.

"I can deal with one neegall," he said.

"The Kantos are planning our annihilation, Gayel. They could send any sort of bug to attack you, our King. If they hurt you, they hurt all of us."

Yes, the Kantos. Gayel felt a pulse of revulsion and anger. The insectoid species had one directive—devour.

They targeted planets, then invaded and consumed. They engineered all manner of ugly, deadly bugs, although the main, four-legged Kantos soldiers were the backbone of the Kantos army.

Recently, they'd targeted a small planet called Earth.

After a string of attacks, Earth had reached out to the Eon. It had been in an unconventional way—one of their Space Corps sub-captains abducting an Eon war commander—but they'd certainly succeeded in getting the Eon's attention.

Gayel's father had been set in his ways. He'd banned contact with Earth decades ago, after first contact with the Terrans had gone badly.

But the Terrans were stubborn, persistent, and resilient.

And Gayel was not his father.

Or at least he worked hard every day not to be.

Needless to say, the Eon Empire and Earth now had an alliance, and beyond that, several Eon warriors were now mated to Terrans.

"Gayel," Adlyn said impatiently. "We need to get back to the palace."

He sighed. Duty called. His father had been a firm and rigid king. Gayel was aiming for firm, but fair. He'd been raised knowing his duty to the Empire, but he was doing things his way.

"The Terran shuttle with your bride candidates is arriving within the hour."

A sensation moved through him, and it wasn't entirely pleasant.

To cement the alliance with Earth, he'd decided to take a Terran bride.

He nodded. "Let's go."

"You're still going ahead with this lunacy?" his sister asked.

"A king needs a queen and an heir. It will bring great stability to the Empire, and a wedding will be a great celebration for our people. Especially now, in the midst of battle with the Kantos."

Adlyn wrinkled her nose. "You sound like father."

Gayel bit back a growl.

"Don't you want to find your mate?" she asked.

His jaw tightened. "Mating is not a luxury a king can afford."

His parents hadn't been mated when they'd first married. It had been an arranged union, although luckily for them, mating had come later. They'd had a content, prosperous marriage.

Mating—where a warrior's helian bonded with his mate as well—had gotten extremely rare for the Eon. Their best scientists had studied the problem to no avail, before turning their attention to medically helping normal, married couples to conceive.

Helians controlled a warrior's fertility, and without a mate, they weren't fertile.

Adlyn was one of the lucky ones—she'd found her mate early. She had a young son, although she'd tragically lost her mate over a year ago.

Gayel and his sister headed back to where he'd left his drail—the massive steeds native to Eon.

Deep inside, Gayel might dream of feeling the mating bond, but he squashed that dream.

As always, he would do his duty.

As for the group of potential brides, he was sure he'd find a kind, compassionate intelligent woman to stand at his side. He'd provide for her, be true to her, and protect her from any danger.

"Any word on the Kantos?" he asked.

His sister scowled and shook her head. "Nothing. It's so quiet, I almost want them to attack."

It might be quiet, but Gayel knew that they weren't gone. They were biding their time, and no doubt planning something.

He already knew they'd been working on a pathogen designed to splinter the bond between warrior and helian. His gut hardened.

He wouldn't let the Kantos continue to kill or harm his people.

War wasn't coming, it was already here.

"We'll be landing soon, Captain."

Captain Alea Rodriguez looked up from the console. "Thanks, Ben."

Finally. She'd be happy to get off the ship and get her charges on the ground.

Her second-in-command, Lieutenant Benjamin Knox, stood in the doorway of the office that Alea had commandeered aboard the *Olympias*. Ben was fifteen years older than Alea, a Space Corps veteran, but had never once been upset reporting to a younger commanding officer. He was fit, had a craggy, rugged face, and graying hair that was cut short. He'd never been married—he maintained that he was married to his career at Space Corps.

Ben was dependable and loyal, and life had taught Alea just how valuable those traits were.

They'd been space marines together, and when Alea had been offered the job as Head of Security at Space Corps Headquarters in Houston two years ago, she'd instantly asked Ben to be her second-in-command.

"You going to tell our charges?" Ben grumbled.

Alea straightened. "You need to hide that sneer a little better, Lieutenant."

Ben's rugged face stayed impassive. "I'll just be happy to spend less time with that group of women."

Alea agreed, although truthfully, the women hadn't been too bad. The group of ten women—Earth's best, brightest, and most beautiful—were all potential candidates for the king of the Eon.

Alea felt like she was on some reality wedding TV show.

Still, she'd seen firsthand what the Kantos could do. Anything that cemented their alliance with the Eon was worth it.

Her gut churned, but she made sure her reaction didn't show on her face. A Kantos strike team had attacked Space Corps Headquarters recently. A teenaged boy had been one of the casualties. He'd died in Alea's arms.

She hadn't been able to save him, nor had she been able to save two members of her security team.

It wouldn't happen again on her watch.

"Alea?"

She looked at Ben, then nodded. "I'll inform the ladies to be ready."

After leaving her office, she straightened her uniform and headed down the corridor of the *Olympias*.

It was a mid-size cruiser with a good crew. It wasn't built for passengers, but she'd made sure the women and the VIPs in their delegation hadn't been uncomfortable.

She paused at the door of the forward observation deck, and heard the murmur of female voices inside. She pressed her palm down on the door control and the door whispered open.

The ten bridal candidates were sitting on low gray couches. When they weren't in their quarters, they were usually here. Some worked, others used the ship's gym.

"Ladies," Alea said.

They were a mix of blondes and brunettes, and one redhead. Some were tall, others short, some were slender, others curvy, their skin tones a range from milky white to gleaming black. Two were successful models—one who also was a designer, while the other ran a skincare and makeup line. There was a doctor, a biologist, a sculptor, two lawyers. A couple of business owners. One ran a nonprofit charity, and the other was an Olympic runner.

King Gayel would have his pick.

"We're in range of the planet Eon, and we'll be boarding a shuttle to the surface soon."

Excited titters filled the room.

"Please have your belongings packed, and on your cabin beds to be taken to the shuttle."

A tall, blonde woman rose. "I need to change. *Finally*, I get to meet the king."

Natasha was one of the models. She was already wearing a tiny, blue dress. Alea had only ever seen the woman in tiny dresses that showed off her mile-long legs. She was the only one as tall as Alea, although Natasha's heels always made her taller.

"You have thirty minutes," Alea warned.

"Yes, Captain." One of the others, Chloe, tossed her a sloppy salute.

God help her. Alea motioned to the large, rectangular window. "In a moment, you'll be able to see the planet."

Sure enough, a few seconds later, the Eon homeworld came into view.

The women rushed to the observation window. Alea took a step closer, as well.

Beautiful.

It was a large, green orb. Eon had fewer oceans than Earth, but from what she'd read, it was covered in lush forests, striking mountains, and jewel-blue lakes.

The capital city of Auris was the crown jewel—a center of commerce, science, and the arts.

Alea was excited to see it.

"My gosh, I could be the queen of that," one of the women said breathlessly.

"No, because I will," another said.

"Ladies, that hunky Eon king is *all* mine. Queen Melinda has a nice ring to it."

They all laughed. Filled with eagerness.

Alea shook her head. There was no way she'd ever be a queen. The daughter of drug dealers wasn't exactly queen material.

She shot one last glimpse at Eon, then strode out.

She was a Space Corps lifer. Being a queen would make her crazy.

Her comm badge chimed and she touched it. "Rodriguez."

"We're entering orbit, Captain."

"Acknowledged."

It was time to pack her own gear. Her thoughts shifted to the powerful king waiting below.

King Gayel Solann-Eon.

He'd visited Space Corps' Headquarters on Earth recently. She'd been so busy overseeing security for his visit that she hadn't met him. She'd only glimpsed him from a distance.

A funny sensation moved through her chest, but she shrugged it off as normal. The guy was gorgeous.

Being a king hadn't made him soft. He was every inch an Eon warrior—tall, broad-shouldered, square jaw, longish brown hair the color of oak.

He had a commanding presence. Even from a distance, the man had radiated authority.

Alea wondered which lucky lady would snag his attention.

She shook her head. *Let's get dirtside, Rodriguez. You have a job to do.*

Over the next thirty minutes, she transferred her duffel bag to the shuttle, oversaw the loading of the women's gear, and got the women on board.

After checking long-range scanners, they got ready to depart.

Thankfully, there was no sign of the Kantos.

She wasn't taking any chances with the women's safety. They would make a nice, juicy target for the Kantos. Alea frowned as she headed into the shuttle bay.

The Kantos had been quiet since their last brazen attack. During that, they'd abducted Medical Commander Thane Kann-Eon of the *Rengard*, and Commander Kaira Chand, a Terran who'd been in charge of security for a secret Terran weapons facility. Luckily, the pair had survived their deadly encounter with the enemy, and ended up mated.

Alea didn't like it. It was highly unlikely that Kantos would be this deep in Eon space, but she had no doubt they'd be busy cooking up something nasty. Fortunately, their escort was the premier warship in the Eon fleet, the *Desteron*.

In the shuttle bay, she noted some *Olympias* crew using what looked like flamethrowers, except they gave off a white mist.

"Ensign?" Alea called out. "What's going on?"

"Captain." The young woman closest to her nodded. "Some bugs from Earth got aboard. The Sub-Captain thinks they got in via the new plants in the hydroponics bay. We're fumigating."

Alea tensed. "You're sure they're from Earth?"

The woman nodded. "Nothing alien has shown up on internal scanners."

Alea relaxed. "Very good." She boarded the shuttle.

A young male pilot spotted her and straightened.

"At ease," Alea said.

Ben stomped aboard behind her and nodded.

Alea checked on her charges in the main cabin. "Everyone strap in. We might encounter some turbulence."

All the women had changed. They wore everything

from pantsuits to flirty dresses, makeup all done, and a cloud of mingled perfumes filled the shuttle.

"We're just waiting on the VIPs and Ambassador Thann-Eon," Ben said.

"I'm here."

A brunette appeared at the shuttle door. A hulking Eon warrior stood beside her and her pregnant belly stretched her shirt.

Alea nodded at War Commander Davion Thann-Eon. The man nodded back and touched his mate's back. The pair had flown over from the *Desteron*.

Eve Thann-Eon, formerly Sub-Captain Eve Traynor, was a legend at Space Corps. The pair were now mated and expecting the first Eon-Terran baby. The woman had since become an ambassador to the Eon Empire.

The three Earth VIPs entered, all wearing suits. They'd won a lottery to select the VIPs to visit Eon. The European delegate was a dashing, handsome politician from France, the Americas' delegate was a retired Army general with snow-white hair and a square jaw from the United States, and the African delegate was a tall, willowy, dark-skinned humanitarian from Kenya.

Alea nodded and waved them through to the cabin. "Please take your seats and strap in."

"Thank you, Captain," Jean-Michel Aubert said with a slow, warm smile.

The man took every chance to flirt with her. She kept her face blank. She had to give the guy credit, despite no encouragement from her, he wasn't deterred.

Behind her, Ben made a choked sound and she resisted the urge to kick him.

"Take it easy," Davion said to Eve.

"Sure." Eve rolled her eyes.

Davion's brows snapped together.

Alea hid a smile. Eve wasn't exactly known for sitting still.

"We'll watch over her, War Commander," Alea said.

Eve scowled. "Don't encourage the man. I'm perfectly capable of taking care of myself."

"I'm heading back to the *Desteron*, but I'll be down for the ball," Davion said.

Eve patted her mate's chest. "Go do your training sessions. I'll be fine."

They kissed.

As Davion circled a muscular arm around his mate, Alea felt a tug of...envy, maybe? Alea hadn't had sex in a long time, so maybe it was just that. And she'd never had time for any sort of long-term relationship.

She wasn't even sure she'd be good at long-term. Letting someone close enough to see your vulnerabilities? Nope, not for her.

"Go." Eve waved her man off, and dropped into a seat. "Pilot, I want a steady ride. This baby is squishing all my internal organs. Don't make it worse."

Alea nodded at the pilot in the cockpit. "You heard the ambassador. Let's have an uneventful trip to the surface. Next up, the capital city of Auris."

Eon Warriors
Edge of Eon
Touch of Eon
Heart of Eon

Kiss of Eon
Mark of Eon
Claim of Eon
Storm of Eon
Soul of Eon
King of Eon
Also Available as Audiobooks!

Want more action-packed science fiction romance? Then check out the first book in *Galactic Gladiators*.

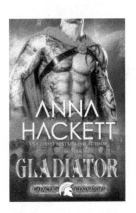

Fighting for love, honor, and freedom on the galaxy's lawless outer rim...

When Earth space marine Harper Adams finds herself abducted by alien slavers off a space station, her life turns into a battle for survival. Dumped into an arena on a desert planet on the outer rim, she finds herself face to face with a big, tattooed alien gladiator...the champion of the Kor Magna Arena.

A former prince abandoned to the arena as a teen, Raiden Tiago has long ago earned his freedom. Now he rules the arena, but he doesn't fight for the glory, but instead for his own dark purpose--revenge against the Thraxian aliens who destroyed his planet. Then his existence is rocked by one small, fierce female fighter from an unknown planet called Earth.

Harper is determined to find a way home, but when she spots her best friend in the arena--a slave of the evil Thraxian aliens--she'll do anything to save her friend...even join forces with the tough alpha male who sets her body on fire. But as Harper and Raiden step foot onto the blood-soaked sands of the arena, Harper worries that Raiden has his own dangerous agenda...

Galactic Gladiators

Gladiator

Warrior

Hero

Protector

Champion

Barbarian

Beast

Rogue

Guardian

Cyborg

Imperator

Hunter

Also Available as Audiobooks!

ALSO BY ANNA HACKETT

Sentinel Security

Wolf

Hades

Striker

Steel

Excalibur

Hex

Also Available as Audiobooks!

Norcross Security

The Investigator

The Troubleshooter

The Specialist

The Bodyguard

The Hacker

The Powerbroker

The Detective

The Medic

The Protector

Also Available as Audiobooks!

Billionaire Heists

Stealing from Mr. Rich

Blackmailing Mr. Bossman

Hacking Mr. CEO

Also Available as Audiobooks!

Team 52

Mission: Her Protection

Mission: Her Rescue

Mission: Her Security

Mission: Her Defense

Mission: Her Safety

Mission: Her Freedom

Mission: Her Shield

Mission: Her Justice

Also Available as Audiobooks!

Treasure Hunter Security

Undiscovered

Uncharted

Unexplored

Unfathomed

Untraveled

Unmapped

Unidentified

Undetected

Also Available as Audiobooks!

Oronis Knights

Knightmaster

Knighthunter

Galactic Kings

Overlord

Emperor

Captain of the Guard

Conqueror

Also Available as Audiobooks!

Eon Warriors

Edge of Eon

Touch of Eon

Heart of Eon

Kiss of Eon

Mark of Eon

Claim of Eon

Storm of Eon

Soul of Eon

King of Eon

Also Available as Audiobooks!

Galactic Gladiators: House of Rone

Sentinel

Defender

Centurion

Paladin

Guard

Weapons Master

Also Available as Audiobooks!

Galactic Gladiators

Gladiator

Warrior

Hero

Protector

Champion

Barbarian

Beast

Rogue

Guardian

Cyborg

Imperator

Hunter

Also Available as Audiobooks!

Hell Squad

Also Available as Audiobooks!

The Anomaly Series

Soul Stealer

Salvation

Anomaly Series Box Set

The Phoenix Adventures

Among Galactic Ruins

At Star's End

In the Devil's Nebula

On a Rogue Planet

Beneath a Trojan Moon

Beyond Galaxy's Edge

On a Cyborg Planet

Return to Dark Earth

On a Barbarian World

Lost in Barbarian Space

Through Uncharted Space

Crashed on an Ice World

Perma Series

Winter Fusion

A Galactic Holiday

Warriors of the Wind

Tempest

Storm & Seduction

Fury & Darkness

Standalone Titles

Savage Dragon

Hunter's Surrender

One Night with the Wolf

For more information visit www.annahackett.com

ABOUT THE AUTHOR

I'm a USA Today bestselling romance author who's passionate about *fast-paced, emotion-filled* contemporary romantic suspense and science fiction romance. I love writing about people overcoming unbeatable odds and achieving seemingly impossible goals. I like to believe it's possible for all of us to do the same.

I live in Australia with my own personal hero and two very busy, always-on-the-move sons.

For release dates, behind-the-scenes info, free books, and other fun stuff, sign up for the latest news here:

Website: www.annahackett.com